I HAVE LOST MY WAY

ALSO BY GAYLE FORMAN

Sisters in Sanity

If I Stay

Where She Went

Just One Day

Just One Year

Just One Night (novella)

I Was Here

Leave Me

Pour Your Heart Out

I HAVE LOST MY WAY

By

GAYLE FORMAN

VIKING

VIKING

An imprint of Penguin Random House LLC

375 Hudson Street

New York, New York 10014

First published in the United States of America by Viking,
an imprint of Penguin Random House LLC, 2018

LIBRARY OF CONGRESS CATALOGING-IN-PUBLICATION DATA IS AVAILABLE.

ISBN 9780425290774

Printed in U.S.A.

Set in Dante

Book design by Nancy Brennan

3   5   7   9   10   8   6   4   2

———o———

For Ken Wright, Anna Jarzab, and Michael Bourret

———o———

Come, come, whoever you are. Wanderer, worshiper, lover of leaving. It doesn't matter. Ours is not a caravan of despair. Come, even if you have broken your vows a thousand times. Come, yet again, come, come.

—Jalaluddin Rumi

———o———

Not all those who wander are lost.

—J. R. R. Tolkien

I HAVE LOST MY WAY

1

I HAVE LOST MY WAY

I have lost my way.

Freya stares at the words she just typed into her phone.

I have lost my way. Where did *that* come from?

"Excuse me, miss," the car service driver repeats. "I think I have lost my way." And Freya startles back to reality. She's in the backseat of a town car on her way to her seventh—or is it eighth?—doctor's appointment in the past two weeks, and the driver has gotten turned around outside the tunnel.

She toggles over to her calendar. "Park and Seventieth," she tells the driver. "Turn right on Third, then left on Seventy-First."

She returns her attention to the screen. *I have lost my way.* Eighteen characters. But the words have the undeniable ring of truth to them, the way middle C does. The way few of her posts these days do. Earlier this morning, someone from Hayden's office put up a photo of her gripping a microphone, grinning. *#BornToSing*, the caption read. *#ThankfulThursday.* Really it should read *#TBT*, because the image is not only weeks old, it's of a person who no longer exists.

I have lost my way.

What would happen if she posted that? What would they say if they knew?

It's only when her phone makes the whooshing noise that Freya realizes she did post it. The responses start to flow in, but before she has a chance to read them, there's a text from her mother: 720 Park Ave, and a dropped pin. Because of course her mother is monitoring the feed as vigilantly as Freya. And of course her mother has misunderstood. Anyway, Freya hasn't lost her way. She's lost her voice.

She deletes the post, hoping it was fast enough that no one screenshot it or shared it, but she knows nothing on the internet ever goes away. Unlike in real life.

Her mother is waiting for her when the car arrives, pacing, holding the test results from the last doctor, which she had to hightail it into the city to collect. "Good, good, you're here," she says, opening the door before the driver has pulled to a complete stop and yanking Freya to the sidewalk before she has a chance to give him the ten-dollar tip she's holding. "I already filled out the paperwork." She says this like she did it to save time, but she fills out the paperwork at all of Freya's doctor's appointments.

They're ushered straight past reception into the examination room. It's the kind of service a $1,500 consult, no insurance taken (thanks, Hayden) buys you.

"What seems to be the problem?" the doctor asks as he

washes his hands. He does not look at Freya. He probably has no idea who she is. He looks old, like a grandfather, though reportedly he has treated the sort of one-named wonder that as of a few weeks ago everyone thought Freya was on her way to becoming.

She wishes she'd read some of the responses before deleting that tweet. Maybe someone would've told her what to do. Maybe someone would've told her it didn't matter if she could sing. They'd still love her.

But she knows that's bullshit. Love is conditional. Everything is.

"She's lost her voice," her mother says. "Temporarily." She goes through the tediously familiar chronology—"third week in the studio" and "all going flawlessly" and *blah blah blah blah*—and all the while the phrase *I have lost my way* goes through Freya's head, like a song on repeat, the way she and Sabrina used to loop the same track over and over again until they'd dissected it, uncovered all its secrets, and made them their own. It drove their mother crazy, until she discovered the utility of it.

The doctor palpates her neck, peers into her throat, scopes her sinuses. Freya wonders how he would respond if she hocked a loogie. If he would actually look at her like a person instead of a piece of machinery that has malfunctioned. If he would *hear* her, singing voice or not.

"Can you sing a high C for me?" the doctor asks.

Freya sings a high C.

"She can hit the individual notes," her mother explains. "And her pitch is perfect. Hayden says he's never heard pitch like that before."

"Is that a fact?" the doctor says, feeling the cords in her neck. "Let's hear a song. Something simple for me, like 'Happy Birthday.'"

"Happy Birthday." Who can't sing "Happy Birthday"? A child can sing "Happy Birthday." A person who can't sing at all can sing "Happy Birthday." To show her opinion of such a request, she starts to sing, but in a heavy French accent.

"*Apee birsday to you . . .*" she trills. Her mother frowns, and Freya doubles down on the accent. "*Apee birsday to vous . . .*"

But her voice is smarter than she thinks. It will not be outsmarted by antics or a bad fake accent. And as soon as the song makes the baby leap in octave, from G4 to G5, she gets tripped up in it. The panic takes over. The breath turns to lead.

"*Appee birsday, dear . . .*" And on the *dear* it happens. The air shuts off. The song is strangled mid-breath. A stillborn melody.

"Happy birthday to me," she finishes in sarcastically atonally American deadpan, making a slicing gesture across her throat in case the message wasn't clear enough.

"Is it paralysis? We heard something like that happened with"—her mother's voice drops—"*Adele.*"

Freya can hear the hope in her mother's voice. Not because she wants vocal paralysis but because she wants to link Freya to Adele. A few years back, she read that book

The Path, and she bought into it 200 percent. *Dream it, be it* is her motto.

"I'm going to send you for some tests," the doctor says, retreating into the already-familiar jargon. "A CAT scan, a biopsy, an LEMG, maybe an X-ray." He pulls out a card, slides it over, and gives Freya a look that does not seem all that Hippocratic. "And you might consider talking to someone."

"We did, but the lobotomy didn't take."

"Freya!" her mother scolds. To the doctor, "We're already seeing a therapist."

We. Like they're seeing him together. Like they're both taking the little pills that are supposed to quell the anxiety that is supposedly stifling Freya's voice.

"This *just* happened. Literally overnight. If this were"— and here her mother's voice drops to a whisper—"*psychological,* it wouldn't happen in the blink of an eye like that, would it?"

The doctor makes noncommittal noises. "Let's schedule a follow-up in two weeks."

Two weeks is too late. Hayden has made that clear. He called in favors to arrange a visit to the famous doctor, treater of one-named wonders like Adele and Lorde and Beyoncé. He paid the $1,500 consultation fee because this guy, Hayden swore, is a miracle worker—implying that what Freya needs is not overpriced medical care but an actual miracle.

Outside, Hayden's car and driver are waiting, even though he didn't send the driver to take Freya here. The driver opens the door and bows slightly. "Mr. Booth has requested I bring you to the offices."

Freya has spent much of the past two years in Hayden's offices, but the request makes her feel queasy. Her mother, who still, after all this time, acts like Hayden is the emperor and she the peasant, looks freaked out. She frantically scrolls through her texts. "He probably just wants to know how it went."

Hayden Booth doesn't summon without reason, and the reason would not be to gather information. Freya's sure he received a call from the doctor the minute the door shut behind them. Or, who knows, maybe he had a secret camera filming the entire exam.

If a tree falls in the forest and no one hears it, does it make a sound? If she doesn't go to Hayden's office, he can't fire her. And if he can't fire her, her career isn't over. And if her career isn't over, people will still love her.

Right?

"I'm tired," she tells her mother, with a weary wave. "You go."

"He asked for us both." She looks to the driver. "Did he ask for us both?"

The driver has no clue. Why would he?

"I'm exhausted from all the stupid doctors' appointments," Freya says, going into what her mother calls diva mode. Diva mode befuddles her mother because on the one hand, *dream it, be it*, but on the other hand, it's fucking annoying.

When her mother gets upset, she purses her lips in a way that makes her look exactly like Sabrina, or Sabrina exactly like her. "It's like the genes chose sides," their old babysitter used to joke. Meaning Freya took after their father—the reddish skin, the high forehead, the telltale Ethiopian eyes— whereas Sabrina looked more like their mother, the hair curly, not kinky, the skin light enough to pass, if not for white, then Puerto Rican.

But then her mother reconsiders, and the prune mouth is gone. "You know what? Maybe that's smarter. I'll talk to him. Remind him that you're only nineteen. That you've come so far. That we have so much momentum. Making them wait will only make them hungrier. We just need a bit more time." She's back on her phone. "I'm ordering you an Uber."

"Mom. I'm quite capable of getting myself back home."

Her mother continues tapping on the phone. Freya's not meant to take the subway alone anymore. Her mother has a tracker installed on Freya's phone. She exercises caution even though, like Freya's diva attitude, this too is premature. Freya is not famous. She is somewhere between buzz and celebrity on Hayden's scale. If she goes dancing at clubs, or hits the kind of bar or café frequented by up-and-coming Actor/Model/ Singers, she's recognized; if she does an event at a shopping mall (which she no longer does; not on brand, the publicists say), she's mobbed. But on the subway, amid regular people, she is exactly nobody. But for her mother, every one of her actions is aspirational.

"I'm just gonna walk a bit," Freya tells her mother. "Maybe go through the park, clear my head, see what's on sale at Barneys."

She knows her mother will not refuse the healing power

of Barneys. Though Freya still feels mildly uncomfortable in places like that. She's often followed, and she is never sure if it's because she's half-famous or half-black.

"Go find something pretty," her mother says. "Take your mind off things."

"What else is on the schedule?" Freya asks, out of habit, because there's always something and her mother has it memorized. Her mother's awkward pause is painful. Because the answer is *nothing*. Nothing is scheduled because this time was allotted to being in the studio. Right now, she's meant to be finishing up recording. Next week, Hayden is going to some private island for a week, and then he's back in the studio with Lulia, the gap-toothed singer he discovered busking in the Berlin metro whom Hayden made so famous that her visage smirks from a billboard in Times Square.

"That could be you," Hayden once told her.

Not anymore.

"Nothing," her mother says.

"So I'll see you back at the apartment."

"Well, it's Thursday."

Thursday nights her mother and Sabrina have a standing dinner date. It usually goes unmentioned. Freya is never invited.

Obviously.

"I can put it off if you need me," her mother says.

The bitterness is awful. She can taste it. She wonders if it'll melt the enamel off her (recently whitened) teeth.

It's also embarrassing. What should she have to be bitter about where her sister is concerned? Sabrina, who, as her mother says, has *sacrificed so much*. She whispers the last part the same way she whispers *breather* when discussing what's going on with Freya. "You're just taking a *breather*."

(*Breather* is code for *self-immolation*.)

"You'd better go," Freya tells her mother before the bitterness melts away her insides, leaving only a bag of empty skin. "Hayden's waiting."

Her mother glances at the SUV, the driver. "I'll call you as soon as I get news." She climbs into the car. "Clear your head. Take a day for yourself. Don't think about any of this. You never know—it might be just what the doctor ordered. I bet if you can go the rest of the day without thinking about this, you'll feel better. Go shopping. Go home and binge *Scandal*."

Yes, that's exactly what Freya needs. And perhaps a glass of warm milk. And a second lobotomy.

She waits for her mother to drive off before she starts walking, not south toward Barneys but west toward the park. She pulls out her phone and looks at her Instagram feed. There's another shot of her, standing outside the studio on Second Ave., under a just-blooming cherry tree. The caption reads, *#Music #Flowers #Life #BeautifulThings*, and the comments are full of nice things that should make her feel better. *Nothing more Btiful than U.* And *NEED NEW VID!* And *Follow-backPLZ!!!!*

A car honks, and someone yanks her back onto the curb,

sneering, "Pay attention." Freya doesn't say thank you, instead walks into the park, where there's no traffic and she can read the comments in peace.

She toggles over to her YouTube channel. Per Hayden's instructions, she has not posted anything in months. He wanted the fans to be "famished" for new material so that when the album dropped, and new videos, they'd be devoured. Freya was worried they'd forget her, but Hayden said there were other ways to stay in the public eye and employed a publicist whose job it was to place a series of anonymous scoops about her.

Freya climbs up a hill, onto a small bridge. A group of cyclists whizzes past her, blasting through the air with their shrill whistles, as if they own the park. She opens Facebook. She types *Sabrina Kebede*. Though she only allows herself this indulgence once a month, Freya knows there won't be anything there. Her sister's Facebook page has been all but dormant for the past two years, maybe two or three posts, almost always tags.

And yet, there it is, a fresh post, a few weeks old. A picture posted by someone named Alex Takashida of a man, presumably Alex Takashida, holding up a delicate hand with a small sapphire ring. The caption underneath reads: *She said yes!*

Even with the face cut off, Freya recognizes that hand.

She said yes! It takes Freya a minute to understand what this means. Her sister is engaged. To Alex Takashida. Someone Freya has never heard of, much less met.

Freya clicks on Alex's timeline and discovers that Alex Takashida makes his posts public, and Sabrina, though not tagged, is in nearly all of them. There's Sabrina clinking glasses with Alex at a restaurant. There's Sabrina and Alex on a beach. There's Sabrina beaming between Alex and their mother. There's Sabrina looking not like someone who *sacrificed so much* but like someone happy.

It makes Freya want to puke. To console herself, she opens the app that tracks what her mother now calls her engagements. She doesn't even need to see the comments anymore to feel better. She just needs to know that they're there. That the likes and follows are growing. The uptick of numbers is reassuring. The occasional downtick makes her feel like her stomach's falling out.

Today, the numbers are going up. Those posts of her in the studio always do well. People are excited about her album. She wonders what will happen when the months go by and there is no album.

Only she knows. At the first meeting with Hayden, he'd told her exactly what would happen.

She opens the comments from this morning's ersatz post. *Love the flowers. Can't wait 4 the album.*♥♥🎻🎸🎵🎧 She refreshes the page to see if anything else has come in but nothing has, and though she knows it'll only make her feel worse, she toggles back to the picture of Sabrina's hand. The cyclists whip by, blowing their awful whistles at her, shouting at her to watch out, but Freya can't take her eyes off her sister and all that happiness. Can't escape the sickening sensation that she's done it all wrong.

I have lost my way, she thinks once more, and understands how true this is. Another cyclist whistles by, and Freya, still staring at the image of her sister's sapphire ring, jumps back and stumbles, and suddenly she is not just lost but falling, falling off the bridge onto some poor soul below.

— — —

Around the time Freya is speaking to yet another doctor who cannot help her, Harun is trying to pray.

As the men stream into the mosque, taking their places, on the rugs around Harun and his father, he tries to make his intention known to God. But for the life of him, he can't. He doesn't know what his intentions are anymore.

He will make for him a way out, his cousin had texted. But what is Harun's way out?

I have lost my way, Harun thinks as the prayer begins.

"*Allahu Akbar,*" he hears his father chant beside him.

And again, the thought: *I have lost my way.* Harun tries to focus. But he can't. He can think of nothing but James.

Forgive me, Harun had texted this morning.

No response.

Not even a *Get the fuck out my life*, which was the last thing James had said to him.

There wouldn't be a response. James never said things he didn't mean.

Unlike Harun.

When the *zuhr* concludes, Harun and his father go outside to collect their shoes and exchange pleasantries with the
other men. All around, there is talk of Hassan Bahara, who
died last week while fueling his car at the gas station.

"It was his heart," Nasir Janjua tells Abu.

Clucking of tongues ensues. Confessions of high choles-
terol levels. Wifely naggings to get more exercise.

"No, no," Nasir Janjua says. "It was a heart defect, silent
until now."

A defect of the heart. Harun knows a thing or two about
those. But unlike Hassan Bahara, his defect isn't silent. He's
known about it for years.

Abu clasps an arm on Harun's shoulder. "Everything okay?"

I have lost my way. He imagines telling Abu this.

But that would only break his father's heart. It was always
a choice of whose to break. As for his own, a foregone con-
clusion. Broken either way. It's what happens with defective
hearts.

"Yeah, Abu, I'm fine," he says.

"You sure?" he asks. "You don't often come to mosque."
There's no reproach in his voice. His older brother Saif
started middle school on the day 9/11 happened, and after
that he began calling himself Steve and refusing to attend
mosque. By the time Harun stopped going, the battle had already been lost. Or won. Depending on how you looked at it.

"I figured since I'm going . . ." he trails off. "Amir goes
every day."

"Yes, your cousin is very devout." Abu ruffles his hair.

"You are a good boy. You have made Ammi very happy."

"And you?"

"Always."

It is for the *always* he's doing this. To continue the always. To never lose the always.

They reach the intersection of Sip and Westside. Harun turns left, in the opposite direction from his house and Abu's store.

"I thought no school today," Abu says, assuming that is where Harun is going.

There's never school on Thursdays. Thursdays are the invisible day added to the weekly schedule last year. Thursdays are their day to be together in Manhattan, where they can slip through the streets like ghosts.

In winter, they meet at Chelsea Market, waltzing through the restaurants they can't afford to eat at while James, who wants to be a chef one day, ogles the fresh pasta, the buttery croissants, the sausages drying from the rafters, and describes all the meals he will cook for them one day. When the weather is warm, they meet under a little arched bridge in Central Park.

They have not missed a single Thursday. Not when a blizzard shut down the aboveground trains, not when James was sick with bronchitis and all Harun wanted to do was get him somewhere warm and dry but for the life of him could not imagine where such a place might be. They'd wound up in a Panera, drinking tea, watching YouTube videos, pretending it was their apartment.

"I'm just going to tie up some loose ends," he tells Abu.

"Don't be late for dinner," Abu says. "Your mother has taken the last two days off work to cook. Your brother is coming. With his wife." His father tries not to frown at the mention of Saif's wife but is not entirely successful.

"I won't be late," Harun says, even though before he left the house, he took his passport and the five hundred dollars cash meant for tomorrow's trip and tucked them into his pocket. It was a rash, last-minute thing to do, but it opened up the possibility of not getting on that plane, of running away for good, in which case he would be very late for dinner.

Coward.

I have lost my way.

He hugs his father goodbye, which isn't something he often does, and he worries that it'll arouse suspicion, but it doesn't, because Abu says only: "Be home in time. You know how your mother gets."

As soon as Abu is safely out of sight, he texts: Going to our place @ park. Meet me there.

At Journal Square, he enters the PATH station. The smell of the tunnels—musty, moldy, redolent of old garages— makes him ache for James.

Everything does.

He takes the train to the terminus at Thirty-Third Street and walks out past the neon signs of the chain clothing stores. In the early days, before they'd learned the secret public spaces in the city, they'd sometimes stopped in one of these shops, trying on all manner of sweaters and trousers neither had any intention of buying, because they could sneak into the same dressing room and, behind those slatted doors, the discarded sweaters at their feet like a camouflage, steal a kiss. Every so often they'd buy something, like the socks Harun is wearing today. They called it rent.

The phone rings in his hand and Harun jumps, hope rushing in like a rising tide, but it's not James.

"I was thinking it might be nice to buy some of that hand cream for Khala," Ammi says, even though there's already a suitcase of gifts for Khala and Khalu, for the cousins, and of course for the prospective families he'd be meeting. "Are you passing by the Hudson?"

Hudson is a mall not far from their house. "Sure," he tells her, because what is one more lie on the steaming pile of them?

"And some ginger. I want to make you some tea for the plane."

"They won't let me bring liquids through security."

"Well, until security," Ammi says. "To keep you in good health."

His throat closes. He is a coward and a liar and a bad son. He hangs up, and a minute later his phone buzzes with a text and he pulls it out, once again full of hope, but it is Amir.

I will see you soon, Inshallah.

Inshallah, he texts back.

He walks into the park, guided by autopilot and hope, to their spot at the bridge. When he sees someone waiting on top, under the cherry tree that, on that last day, they kissed under, his hope surges again. It could be him, he tells himself, even though the skin is too light and the frame is too small and also it is a woman. If only James were a woman. Ha.

I'm here, he texts.

There is no answer, but that doesn't stop him from seeing James everywhere. There he is, riding a bike in spandex, though James would be horrified by anyone even picturing him in such a ridiculous getup. There he is pushing a baby in a jogging stroller, though James hates exercise. There he is coming toward him, through the tunnel under the bridge.

None of these people are James, and for that, Harun hates them. He hates everything and everyone in this world. If Allah made the world, why did he make Harun wrong? If Allah is love, then why isn't James the one walking through the tunnel instead of some white boy?

This is what he's thinking at the exact moment the girl who is not James falls off the side of the bridge, landing with a loud thud on the boy who is also not James.

— — —

Around the time Freya is speaking to yet another doctor who cannot help her, and Harun is trying to pray, Nathaniel is emerging onto a crowded Manhattan street with no idea of where he is.

"I have lost my way," he says as people stream by him. When no one responds, he isn't that surprised. He's been invisible for a while.

He's followed the directions exactly as the sign at the airport told him to. Walked to the edge of the terminal, climbed on the bus bound for Manhattan. But he must've fallen asleep, because he awoke to the hiss of the bus's pneumatic door and everyone else had filed out.

He tries to focus, but he's disoriented and bleary. The name of the flight he was on, a red-eye, turned out to be literal.

The night before, as the plane sped past the quilt of a country Nathaniel never got to know, around him people snored away wearing sleep masks and neck pillows, taking pills to trick themselves into thinking they were home in bed. But he hadn't slept in the past two weeks, so there seemed little chance he was going to sleep on the plane. After take-off, the passenger in front of him tilted his seat back, sending Nathaniel's knees to his chest. He'd stayed up half the night reading his father's copy of *The Lord of the Rings*, and when he could stand that no more, the guidebook he'd stolen from the library. In the dim cabin light, he learned about sights he would not see. The Empire State Building. The Metropolitan Museum of Art. Central Park. The Botanical Gardens. He flipped through the index, looking at the piece of paper he'd taken from his father. Their meeting point.

Out in the daylight, Nathaniel blinks and tries to orient himself. Everything is so new and so different. The buildings taller than the tallest trees. The light unrestrained by clouds, the sound so loud he has to close his eyes to be able to process it (there, the thumping bass of reggae music; there, the distant sound of jackhammers; there, voices arguing; there, a baby crying). After so much silence, he has auditory culture shock, if such a thing exists.

He's jolted back to the moment when someone pushes past him. It's a rude gesture, a New York gesture, even, but he relishes the human touch. He's been alone for two weeks, but it might as well be an eternity, and he'll take what he can get.

Still, when another passerby hisses at him to move it, he does. He retreats out of the flow of traffic, under an awning. From here, he can watch. There are people, more people that he's ever seen in one place, doing everything fast, from smoking cigarettes to having animated conversations on their cell phones. No one looks at him.

He didn't really consider this. The people. The city. A rush of regret because he won't have time to experience it. Now, where is he meant to be going again? The subway, an alphabet soup of letters and numbers. His was easy. The A train. According to the map at the airport, the bus should've dropped him off right on the corner where the subway was supposed to be. But he's not on the corner, but in the middle of a long block. He walks to the nearest corner. The street sign reads: *Forty-Second Street.* Across the street is a park, a patch of green amid the skyscrapers. Which is nice, unexpected— even the park seems surprised to find itself here—but that doesn't help him figure out where he is and where he's supposed to be.

"I have lost my way," he says to the stream of pedestrians. "Can anyone tell me where the A train is?"

But they keep moving, a million-limbed organism rather than individual people, and then there's Nathaniel, the amputee.

On the plane, in the guidebook, he'd read that Manhattan was a grid, avenues running north-south, streets east-west, street numbers going higher as you go north, the avenues dividing into east and west with Fifth Avenue running down the middle like a spine. If you were lost, the book said, the landmarks could help you get your bearings: the Twin Towers to the south, the Empire State Building to the north.

The Twin Towers, he knows, are gone. It's a sort of hubris to put something like that in a book as a landmark, a guidepost, to assume it will always be there.

"One day we'll go to New York City," his father had promised him, scratching it onto the list on the inside wall of his closet. "One day we'll go to Mount Denali," his father had promised him.

"What about the Shire?" Nathaniel had asked when he was too little to know the difference between places real and imagined.

"Sure," his dad had promised. "We'll go there too."

Yellow taxis pass by, looking like they did in the TV shows he and his father used to occasionally watch in between the documentaries. He could just take a taxi to his final destination. He pulls out his wallet, furtively counting the rest of his cash (the guidebook warned: "Be wary of pickpockets and scam artists"). After emptying out the bank account, there had been enough money for the plane ticket, the bus fare to and from the airport, and about a hundred and twenty bucks left over. Part of him had known that going anywhere, let alone New York City, with so small a cushion was folly. But that was just the point. Remove the net. Eliminate the possibility of backtracking.

Still, after so long being prudent and frugal, he can't completely shed his old ways. He decides against getting a taxi. He has no idea how much the trip will cost. He smells like country, like a rube, and maybe the driver will rip him off. ("Be wary of pickpockets and scam artists.") And besides, he doesn't know how to make a taxi stop. He sees how other people do it, stepping into the street, sticking out a hand, but suspects if he did that, the cars would pass right by.

He pulls out his phone, missing his father so much it aches. He dials the number. Three rings before the call goes to voicemail. "Tell me something good," his father's recording says.

"Hey, Dad," Nathaniel says. "I made it."

He hangs up the phone, opens the guidebook, and thumbs through for the big map in the middle. He finds Forty-Second Street and draws a line across it until he finds a square block of green, amazed, relieved, ebullient, even, that there's some representation, some proof, of where he is.

The patch of green is Bryant Park. Sixth Avenue, which runs up the west side of the park, dead-ends at Central Park. Central Park! That was one of the places in the book. To the left of the park he sees the big blue circle for the A train. He could walk there. Why not?

He sets off, feeling the same lightness he'd experienced when he'd made the decision to come here. He passes Fiftieth Street, the signs blaring for Rockefeller Center, more people crossing at a single intersection than in his entire graduating class. He passes Fifty-Fourth Street and sees signs for the Museum of Modern Art, and though he's not visiting it, he feels like he's seen some of it. ("One day we'll see the *Mona Lisa*," his father had promised, and though Nathaniel is fairly certain the *Mona Lisa* is not here, it still feels like he has made a little good on that promise.)

He gets to Central Park faster than he thought. Too fast. He can see that the western edge reaches the big circle where the A train is, but he opens up the map in his book again. The park itself runs to 110th Street. He can walk there. Or all the way up. On the bus before he'd fallen asleep, he'd caught a glimpse of the looming Manhattan skyline from across the river just before they'd entered the tunnel. It seemed inconceivable that he could breach such a fortress, but here he is. He can afford to take his time. His father will understand.

Entering the park, he's surprised by how familiar it seems. It's an entirely different kind of nature from what he grew up in, but it turns out that trees are trees, flowers are flowers, birds are birds, wind is wind.

Overhead, the sun is a little west of high noon. He knows where he is. He knows which way is north. He abandons the main roadway for one of the smaller paths. He might get a little lost, but the sleep has shaken away from him. He feels more awake and alive than he has in days. He knows where he's going.

The path winds under a small arched bridge, a tunneled portal into the park. He examines the bricks. They're so old, the keystone binding the two seams is almost invisible. Under the bridge the air is dark and musty. He holds his breath, like he used to when they would drive through tunnels, his father encouraging him in the longer ones (*You're almost there, buddy*).

I'm almost there, he tells his father as he steps out of the tunnel. He feels a rush of air that turns out to be Freya falling, but he doesn't have time to see that, much less comprehend it, because she has landed on top of him and everything has gone black.

THE ORDER OF LOSS
PART I

FREYA

When I was one minute old, I sang my first song. That was the story my father told me. When I was born, I didn't cry or make a sound, and for a minute, my father said, his heart stopped because he thought there was something wrong with me. All the doctors and nurses swooped in. Then I made a noise, not a baby noise, not a cry or a grunt, but something undeniably musical. "It was a perfect A sharp," my father told me, sustained for at least a second or two. The medical personnel all started laughing in relief. "You were born singing," my father told me. "And you haven't stopped since."

"That's dumb," my sister Sabrina declared. "Babies aren't born doing anything, let alone singing." But she just said that because she was jealous. Our father hadn't been in the delivery room when she was born four years before me. He was out playing a gig, and by the time he got word Mom was in labor, Sabrina had already arrived, and though nobody reported it, I would guess she was born not singing but scowling.

Maybe because he was in the delivery room, maybe because I was born singing, or maybe because we looked alike, I belonged to my father, and Sabrina to my mother. It was almost like they decided on a split-custody arrangement before they even got divorced. Sabrina would spend her evenings with Mom, doing crossword puzzles or rearranging the kitchen cabinets. I would spend my afternoons with my father, huddled in the tiny closet he used as a studio. There, amid boxes of old LPs and cassettes, he would play me recordings of his favorite artists: American singers like Billie Holiday and Nina Simone and Josephine Baker, and Ethiopian singers like Aster Aweke and Gigi. "Hear how they sing their sorrows? How they sing what they can't say?" He'd show me pictures of these women, who had beautiful voices and beautiful faces. "Blessed twice like the jacaranda tree," he'd say. "Like you."

There were no jacaranda trees in White Plains, where we lived at the time, but my father had already told me about how in spring in Addis Ababa, they bloomed with magnificent blossoms, purple and fragrant, blessed twice. He told me about how in winters, which were cold but nothing like here, the air filled with the smell of eucalyptus smoke. He told me of his mother's cooking, which he missed so much. The *tibs* she would make for him, the *shiro*, the goat they would roast before the fasting holidays, the fermented *injera* bread. He took me into the city to restaurants that served his favorite foods, which became my favorite foods. He let me sip the bitter coffee and the sweet honey wine. He showed me how to eat with my fingers, not dropping any bits. *"Konjo, konjo,"* the waitresses who looked like me would say to him. "Beautiful."

He promised one day he would take me to Ethiopia with him. He promised one day he would take me to the clubs in New York City where once upon a time Charlie Parker, Miles Davis, and John Coltrane had played. He promised one day he'd take me to hear his hero, the Ethiopian jazz musician Mulatu Astatke, whose career he had moved to America to emulate. "People thought it was not possible to combine the Ethiopian and the American, but listen to the proof," he would say, playing me recordings of Astatke. "And look at the proof," he would say, smiling at me.

"Sing with me, Freaulai," he would say, and I would sing. And whenever I did, he closed his eyes and smiled. "Born singing."

"Be quiet!" my sister would call from the other room. Like my mother, she had no interest in Astatke or *tibs* or ever going to Ethiopia. "We live here," they would tell my father when he mused about moving us home, nearer to his family. "We are your family," they would tell him.

"Stop singing!" Sabrina would yell if I didn't shut up.

"Promise me you'll never stop singing," my father would whisper to me.

I promised. Unlike him, I kept my promises.

— — —

Sabrina claimed that once upon a time, our parents laughed together and danced in the living room. That Mom used to go to our father's gigs, googly-eyed, convinced that love could overcome the wide gap between a Jewish girl from Westchester and a jazz musician from Addis.

Sabrina said that all changed when I came along. Was this true? Or was this Sabrina being Sabrina? Sabrina, who would squeeze my wrist until she left red marks. "Love twists," she called them, to remind me who loved me. Sabrina, who would whisper in my ear: "Your breath stinks. Your hair is nappy," and who grew angry if I cried. "If people who love you can't tell you the truth, who can?" she'd say.

As for my parents once loving each other, I couldn't say. The staccato beat and locked horns of their fights were nearly as constant a soundtrack to my childhood as the music my father played me. Though like so many things, I didn't really realize this until the sound stopped and silence engulfed us.

— — —

When I was ten years old, I came home from school one day to find my father awake, which was unusual enough. He was a driver for a car service at night in the city, getting off late and trying to get a minute or two on stage somewhere at the dwindling number of clubs in the Village. He often came home as Sabrina and I were getting up for school and slept until it was time to work again that evening. But that day, he was up. The table was set with the round platters of Ethiopian food.

I was so excited by the meal and my father being home that I failed to notice his packed bag and trumpet case in the hall. But I wouldn't have thought much of it. It was not unusual for my father to go on short tours, though it hadn't happened for a few years.

"Where are you going?" asked Sabrina, who had noticed.

"My mother is sick," he replied, serving us big portions of food. "I am going home to visit her."

"Will she be okay?" I asked. I had never met Ayate. She was too frail to travel, and my mother said we didn't have enough money to afford the tickets to Ethiopia.

"She will be fine," my father said.

"When are you coming back?" Sabrina asked.

"Soon, Sipara."

Sabrina frowned. She did not like it when he used her Ethiopian name. "How soon?" she asked.

"Soon," he repeated. "Is there anything you want me to bring back?"

"Will you bring us one of those white dresses?" I asked. I'd seen them on the women at the restaurant and in the pictures of my cousins. They were beautiful, gauzy and white, with delicate embroidery. I desperately wanted one.

"A *habesha kemis*?" He smiled. "I promise." He looked at Sabrina. "Do you want me to bring you one?"

"No, thank you."

We finished eating and he stood to leave. He had tears in his eyes as he held me close and sang to me, not the Billie Holiday or Nina Simone songs we sang together but "Tschay Hailu," the rhythmic lullaby he used to sing to me every night. *Eshururururu, eshururururu, ye binyea enate tolo neyelete dabowen baheya wetetune beguya yezeshelet neye yezeshelet neye.*

"Sing with me, Freaulai," he said, and I did.

When the song was over, he pushed me away to arm's length, tears streaming down his face. "Promise me you will never stop singing."

I said what I always said—that I promised.

He wiped his face, picked up his suitcase and trumpet, and left. I chased him to the hallway. "Don't forget the white dress," I called.

But he was already gone.

— — —

My grandmother died five weeks later. I cried, not because I was sad but because my father would be staying for the funeral and to settle her affairs. And the weeks without him had already been enough. With him absent, my family was like a three-legged chair.

"How much longer?" I asked over the crackling phone line when he'd been gone two months.

"Not much longer," he said.

"And you won't forget the white dress?"

"I won't forget."

I hung up the phone. Sabrina was standing there. She had spoken to him for only a few moments, monosyllabic yes/no answers. It was like she didn't miss him at all. But why should she? She belonged to our mother, and our mother was still here.

She had her arms crossed in front of her chest and was looking at me with the same mean expression she wore when

she pointed out some flaw of mine. "You know he's not coming back, right?"

"What are you talking about?"

"He's home now," she said. "He doesn't want to come
back."

"But we're here."

"Mom was going to kick him out anyway," Sabrina said.
"You think he'd come back just for you?"

"You're just being mean."

She looked at me. She was fourteen years old, but she already had a stare that could make a grown-up flinch. "He
took his trumpet, Freya. Why would he take his trumpet if
he was coming back?"

"Maybe he wanted to play music for Ayate," I said.

"He's not coming back," Sabrina said.

"Yes he is!" I screamed at her. "You're just jealous because
he loves me more. Because I can sing. He's coming back!"

She didn't even seem mad. She looked at me almost pity-
ingly. Because she knew. Sabrina always knew.

"No, he's not."

— — —

A few months after that I received a package in the mail. The
stamps bore the squiggly, indecipherable writing of Amharic
and showed that the package had been mailed weeks before.

Inside was a white dress. It was beautiful. Gauzy, embroi-
dered with purple and gold thread. It fit me perfectly. There
was a note from my father. *I promised*, it said.

And that was when I knew Sabrina was right.

I threw the dress into the trash. Then I went to my room and climbed into bed and began to cry.

"What's gotten into you?" Mom asked when she found me there that night. It was still several weeks before she would sit me and Sabrina down in a booth at the Star Diner and solemnly announce what we already knew: that she and our father were getting divorced; that he was staying in Addis for the foreseeable future, but they'd work something out so we could go visit. Another promise unkept.

I didn't answer. I just kept crying into my pillow.

"I don't know what's with her," I heard my mother tell Sabrina. "Or how to snap her out of it."

That was my father's job. He was the one who sat with me when I was sick or scared. He was the one who didn't ask for explanations when sometimes I was just so overcome with emotions I didn't know what to do. "Sing what you can't say, Freaulai," he would say.

I was still crying when I heard the door creak open. It was not my mother, who had come in several times and admonished me to cut it out. It was Sabrina.

Silently, she climbed into the bed, and then my sister, who did not like to be hugged or kissed or even touched, wrapped her body around mine. "Don't worry," she murmured. "I'll take care of you now."

But I didn't believe her. Sabrina, who delivered love pinches and scathing critiques. Who hated *shiro* and *tibs* and told me to be quiet when I sang. How would she take care of me?

As if she heard my doubts, my sister began to sing to me. *Eshururururu, eshururururu, ye binyea enate tolo.* I had never heard my sister sing, not even on holidays. I didn't know she could sing. And yet she sang the lullaby in a clear, pure voice. She sang it as if she too had been born singing.

"Sing with me," she said.

And I did. *Eshururururu, eshururururu, sefecheme azeyea segagere azeyea seserame azeyea sehedeme azeyea yenima biniyea werede ke jerbayea.* We lay together, singing, harmonizing without even trying. Our voices blended perfectly, easily, in a way that in real life we never did.

We sang and I stopped crying. I believed that as long as we sang together, I would be okay.

THE ORDER OF LOSS
PART II

HARUN

When I was nine, Ammi announced that her sister's family from Pakistan was coming to visit. I was very excited. I'd never met Khala and Khalu or my three cousins. Usna was nineteen, too old to be of interest, but the twins, Amir and Ayisha, were my age. Ayisha was loud and rebellious and made fast friends with my younger sister, Halima, sneaking off to the 7-Eleven, buying Little Debbie snack cakes and Doritos.

That left me with Amir, who was small, quiet, and circumspect, the opposite of his sister. He did not want to go to the movies or play miniature golf or even venture into Manhattan to see the sights. So we stayed around the house, playing board games or lying on our backs in the yard, watching the planes take off from Newark Airport. "That's Continental Airlines flight seventeen, bound for Los Angeles," I told Amir. When he asked how I knew, I showed him the notebook I kept with all the flight departures and arrivals. I'd kept it hidden since Saif had warned me that if anyone saw it, they'd get the wrong idea. But Amir didn't think the notebook was weird, and when I confessed my dream of one day being a pilot, he didn't think that was crazy either. "You can fly to Pakistan and visit me," Amir told me.

Amir went to prayer with his father every day, and that week I joined them even though I normally only went with Abu on Fridays and holidays.

"Your cousin is making you devout," Abu said.

"Your cousin is turning you into a kiss-ass," Saif said.

One day, I came back from mosque to find Ammi and Khala sitting at the dining room table, where Ammi often worked. Her ledgers were spread out, her cup of tea steaming. Khala was complaining about Ayisha, who had been sneaking junk food and hiding the evidence in the trash, where Ammi discovered it because Ammi discovered everything, be it missing receipts or misbehaving children.

"She's already so fat," Khala said, shaking her head.

"She should not lie," Ammi said, inputting a receipt and transferring it from one pile to the other.

"I'm less worried about the lying than her getting fat," Khala replied. "More fat."

Ammi clucked her tongue.

"She's already at a disadvantage," Khala continued. "Amir must have sucked all the beauty away from her when they were in the womb. It would be easier to find Amir a husband than Ayisha."

I didn't totally understand what they were talking about,

but the idea of Amir finding a husband gave me a strange tickling in my tummy.

After that, I could not stop sneaking looks at Amir. He *was* pretty. He had long eyelashes that were apparently enviable and hair that made a little exclamation point in the middle of his forehead, and his lips were red and shiny, the way Halima's were when she sneaked on the berry lip gloss she kept hidden in her backpack. I watched how his lips formed a bow when he drank soda through a straw, and I imagined what it might be like to be that straw between Amir's lips.

"*What?*" Amir asked, catching me staring at him drinking a Sprite.

And there it was, that tickling feeling.

During '*Asr* the next day, I found myself drifting, murmuring the prayers while staring at my cousin's ear. How had I never noticed ears before? The intricacies, the folds, the delicate pearl of the lobes, which on some people, like Abu, stuck to the neck, while on others, like Amir, were unattached. I touched my own ear as if for the first time, and the tickling feeling returned.

That night, we all watched a movie. We chose *Aladdin*, because the cousins had never seen it. Khalu disapproved of the way Islam was depicted. "Also," Amir added, "with how immodestly Jasmine is dressed."

We all huddled around the television in the basement and turned on the TV. The older kids seemed bored by it. Saif kept trying to do all the Robin Williams parts, but it had been a long time since he'd last seen the movie and he kept messing up.

"Shh!" I said, on behalf of the cousins.

"This movie sucks," my brother Abdullah said.

"It's giving me flashbacks," Saif said. "I used to have such fantasies about Jasmine."

"This is not appropriate talk for the children," Usna said primly.

"They don't even know what we're talking about," Saif said.

I do, I wanted to say. Only I didn't. Not entirely, though I felt certain it was tied up with Ammi and Khala's conversation about Amir, and with the strange tickling in my stomach.

I knew Jasmine was meant to be pretty and her manner of dress sexy, and I knew she was an object of desire by the way my brother was talking. But I didn't care about Jasmine. It was Aladdin I couldn't take my eyes off of. His face was pretty, delicate, kind of like Amir's. And the scenes with Aladdin bare-chested made that tickling in my belly stronger than ever.

We finished *Aladdin* and started watching *The Little Mermaid*, but the DVD was scratched, and halfway through we gave up and went to bed.

We had shuffled around to accommodate everyone's sleeping arrangements. Amir and I had been relegated to a leaking blow-up mattress in the living room. We'd been sleeping there all week and nothing had happened, save for a crick or two in my neck.

That night, I dreamed of Aladdin. We were on a carpet,

only not the one from the movie but one from the mosque. I could smell the musky scent of it in the dream.

Aladdin was bare-chested, and I was running my hand over his smooth skin. And he was not a cartoon; he was real. In the dream, Aladdin became Amir. And we were flying. And I was holding on to Amir as Jasmine had done to Aladdin.

The mattress shifted. I opened my eyes slightly, and the tickling sensation blossomed into something stronger, a tingling over my entire body, a throbbing between my legs.

A cool breeze rustled through a gap in the window, and I opened my eyes all the way and saw that in sleep, I had wrapped myself around Amir. My hand was on his chest, warm and sticky. My heart felt full. I understood in that moment that this was who I was.

The mattress moved again, and Amir opened his eyes. "What—?" he began to ask, in that same guilty way he'd asked earlier when he thought he was about to be chastised for drinking too much soda. He looked at my hand. "What are you doing?"

I snatched my hand away. "Mosquito," I lied.

He rolled over and went back to sleep, but I lay in bed rigid, afraid that if I got too close, he would know, as I suddenly knew, that there was something very wrong with me. The next night, I moved to the couch, claiming Amir kicked, and after that I rebuffed his requests to do more plane-spotting. He seemed hurt, but hurt was better than disgusted.

The Friday after the cousins left, Abu asked me if I wanted

to go to *'Asr* again. I liked going to mosque with him, having time alone with him. But I'd been taught that Allah could see into our hearts. He would see me. I knew I couldn't let that happen. I told Abu that I didn't want to go anymore.

Abu sighed and frowned, but he didn't argue. Saif had paved the road for me. He thought I was just being rebellious. I was just being American. I let him think that.

It was the first time I lied to him.

THE ORDER OF LOSS
PART III

NATHANIEL

When I was seven years old my father read me *The Lord of the Rings* for the first time.

"Don't tell your mother," he whispered.

"Why is he still awake?" my mother would complain when a half hour later we were still reading, and I was more keyed up than ever, visions of orcs and elves swimming in my head. "You're supposed to be putting him to sleep."

Then my father would conceal the book under the covers and wink at me. "You and me," he'd whisper after she'd left. "Like Frodo and Sam."

"A fellowship," I'd reply, giggling.

"A fellowship of two." He reached for a pen and scratched some note into the margin of his book before hiding it under my bed.

A fellowship of two—and Mom. The two of us wandering through the forest, looking for edible mushrooms one day, ents the next. The two of us staying out all night to catch a lunar eclipse (unseen, thanks to the omnipresent clouds).

The two of us climbing trees, or building forts, or taking off on an impromptu road trip, never mind that there was school and we hadn't brought any extra clothes. "Why do we need that, buddy?" Dad would say. "We have each other. We're all we need."

When Mom announced that she was leaving, I wasn't even that sad. We had each other, after all.

"I'm so sorry, Nathaniel," she told me. "But I can't live with two children anymore." She wanted me to move with her to California, where it was sunny. "Doesn't that sound nice?" No, it did not. I didn't want to go to California. I wanted to stay here, in my house, with my friends and my father. We were a fellowship, after all.

"I'm not leaving you alone with that man-child," my mother said, and when I told Dad about that, he asked Grandma Mary to come live with us.

"And if she's so mature, why's she runnin' off on an eight-year-old lad?" Mary asked the day she moved in, dropping her flowered suitcase on the entry hall floor and extracting a pair of rubber gloves from her pocketbook, as if anticipating, correctly, the pile of dirty dishes in the sink. "Never you mind," she told me as she scrubbed three-day-old scrambled egg off a plate. "I brung up your father, and I'll bring up you." She glanced at my father, who was on the sofa in his pajamas, reading the funny pages. "Bring up both of you, it seems."

Dad winked at me, and I knew what he was thinking without him saying it. It was Just Us. A fellowship of two.

Once Grandma Mary moved in, she took over what had

been my parents' bedroom, and Dad moved into the spare bed in my room. And just like that, he seemed to fully relinquish a role that had never fully fit in the first place. No more father and son, now we were truly a fellowship. We would stay up late in the night, talking about anything and everything: Was there intelligent life out there? Dad was sure of it. And could it be that we weren't really living but were part of some video game someone else was playing? Dad thought it was a possibility. We talked about the places we might go one day. Dad wanted to see the hidden temples of Angkor Wat. I wanted to go to New York City because I'd started staying up to watch *SNL* and wanted to see it filmed.

"Done and done," Dad promised, adding the places to our list. "We'll do it all. We'll see the world, together."

"A fellowship of two," I said.

It went on like this for years. I lived my life, went to school, and played soccer in the fall, baseball in the spring. I was getting pretty good as a pitcher and a first baseman, and the coach said I might get into a traveling league. Grandma Mary did the grocery shopping and cleaning and took care of me and Dad.

Dad still worked as an IT guy, but he didn't have a steady job anymore; he was what he called a freelancer. Mom called it something else, but after a few years she remarried and had another kid, and stopped complaining about how much Dad worked, stopped asking me if I wanted to come live with her in California.

Grandma Mary was a creature of habit. She wore the

same smocked apron every day. She went to the same mass every Sunday. She smelled of Nivea and Palmolive, and she always coughed. So no one noticed at first when the coughing got worse, more hacking and wet. And no one noticed the blood-speckled tissues that Grandma Mary coughed into, because she flushed them down the toilet.

When she caught a cold that turned into pneumonia, a chest X-ray revealed lung cancer. Stage four, the doctors said.

I had a teammate named Tyler whose uncle had recently died of colon cancer. He was the one who told me what stage four meant. Dad refused to believe it. He insisted Mary would be okay. "Not with stage four she won't," Tyler said.

"My dad's going to figure it out," I told Tyler, because that's what Dad had insisted. He spent hours on the internet, ordering healing crystals one day and shark-fin powder the next. At one point, he was all set to charge airplane tickets to Israel, where some new stem cell treatment was being offered, only to be stymied when the charge was declined.

"She's going to beat this," he insisted.

Meanwhile, Mary grew sicker. She underwent two rounds of chemotherapy and then put a stop to it. "How can I take care of you two if I'm running for the toilet every five minutes?" she asked.

One day, I came home from baseball practice to find Grandma Mary collapsed on the floor. Dad sat beside her, legs crossed, holding her hand, tears streaming down his face.

"Is she dead?" I asked.

"I don't know, I don't know," Dad replied.

I rushed to her, put a finger on her neck as I'd seen done on TV, and felt a pulse there. I was only eleven years old, but I stayed calm, like I already knew what to do, like I'd been preparing for this moment.

When the paramedics arrived, one of them asked, "How long has she been unresponsive?"

I looked at Dad, who was sitting in that same place on the floor, even though he was in the paramedics' way. "How long?"

"I don't know. I don't know," Dad replied, swaying back and forth.

Mary stayed in the hospital for three weeks. The doctors said she probably wouldn't leave.

"Like hell she won't," Dad said. And he insisted on bringing her home. "What she needs is to be out of this institution, away from all those poisons they're pumping into her."

Mary was in no place to make such a decision; Dad was the official adult. The doctors had no choice but to listen to him.

But it was me who met with the hospice coordinator. Who filled out all the paperwork, who got Dad to sign on the dotted line, who arranged for a hospital bed to be delivered to our house and for the hospice nurse to visit.

The hospice nurse was named Hector. He came nearly every day that whole summer Mary lay dying, at first just for an hour or so to adjust her pain meds and make sure she was comfortable.

"Where's your father?" he would ask me on the days when Dad was absent.

"Oh, at work," I would lie. I didn't know where Dad was. Out on a walk. Playing pool. Hunting for the cure for cancer out in the woods.

As Grandma Mary grew sicker, Hector stayed longer and longer, all afternoon, even toward the end when all she did was sleep. Sometimes he lingered in the kitchen with me, once frying me what looked like a green banana but turned out to be something called a plantain, and which was delicious. Other times, he sat with Mary, rubbing lotion onto her hands, combing her hair, talking to her, singing to her.

"Can she hear you?" I asked him once.

"I believe she can." He beckoned me closer. I didn't like to be in the sick room. It smelled sour, like slightly off milk, and Mary made a terrible rattling sound as she labored for breath. But with Hector I didn't feel so scared.

I stood by his side as he ministered to my grandmother. The look on his face was serene, even happy. I didn't understand. "Isn't it sad watching so many people die?" I asked.

"We all die," Hector said, rubbing Mary's wrists. "It's the only sure thing in life and the one thing we have in common with everything else on the planet." He let go of her hand and put it in mine. I could feel her pulse, rabbity and weak.

"I think it's an honor to be with people as they leave the world," he told me.

"An honor?"

"An honor," he replied. "And a calling. You know, I was about your age when I realized I wanted to do this."

"Really?"

"Maybe not so concretely, but yes. I was with my own grandmother when she was dying. This was back home in Washington Heights, in New York City. She had barely spoken in weeks, but right before she passed, she sat up and came alive, carrying on a two-hour conversation with someone in the room. In Spanish. And I didn't really speak Spanish, so I knew she wasn't talking to me."

"Who was she talking to?"

"Only she knew for sure, but I felt certain it was my grandfather. He'd been dead for twenty years. I never even met him. But at that moment, I knew he was in the room with her, there to escort her to what was next."

Chills went up my spine.

"I've seen this happen more times than I can count," Hector continued. "The dying speaking to the dead. The dead leading the dying to what's next."

"What *is* next?" I asked.

He smiled. "That I don't know. And unfortunately, none of us finds out until it's our turn, and then we're in no position to report back."

Two weeks later, Grandma Mary died quietly. If someone came to escort her to what was next, they did so silently.

"It's just us," my father said when they took Mary's body away. Only for the first time it felt less like a promise than a threat.

2

IT'S ALL GOOD

It's all good, Nathaniel tries to say.

Only he can't seem to talk. Or move. Or think too clearly. Or see the shadowy person hovering over him, stroking his forehead, asking him to please, please wake up.

The stroking feels nice, though.

Everything else, not so nice.

"Can you hear me?" the voice asks. "Can you move?"

It's a beautiful voice. Even in his current state he can hear this. If a voice could emit a scent, this one would smell like dates.

Grandma Mary used to buy dried dates. They ate them and spat the pits into the yard, hoping a date tree would grow, but dates grow in the desert, and he lives in the forest.

Lived in the forest.

There's breath against his neck, whispery and warm. The breath says: "Open your eyes. Wake up."

"Please," the breath says.

It's the *please* that does it. There's something so raw, so plaintive in it. How can he not obey?

He opens his eyes. A pair of eyes stare back at him. They are maybe the loveliest eyes he's ever seen. And the saddest. So sad, they could be his eyes, except they are brown and his eyes—eye—is green.

"What's your name?" the Stroker whispers into his ear. And that voice. It sends a shiver down his spine, not because it's beautiful, smelling of dates, but because it's familiar, and it can't be familiar because he doesn't know a soul in . . . where is he? It doesn't matter. He doesn't know a soul in the world with a voice like that.

"What's your name?" the voice repeats.

His name. He knows his name. It's just there, on the highest shelf in the back of the closet. He's got to reach for it. It's . . .

"Nathaniel," the voice says. "Nathaniel Haley. Is that you?"

Yes! That's him! Nathaniel Haley. How does she know?

"From Washington State."

Yes! he wants to shout. From a house on the edge of a forest that's been swallowed up. How does she know?

"And you just arrived here . . . today."

Yes. Yes. Yes. But how does she know?

"Welcome to New York," she says. "Pro tip: Don't leave your wallet in your pocket. Any old person can get it."

His wallet. He tries to summon it. He sees a billfold. A picture.

"Can you sit up?" the Stroker asks. Nathaniel doesn't want to sit up, but there are those fingertips, and that voice, calling,

Nathaniel, Nathaniel, come back. And that voice, so familiar it's like an itch, and so beautiful, it's like a song. He can heave himself up. To see the voice.

For one lovely moment, it's worth the effort, to be face-to-face with that face. Until . . .

The pain is on a delay, and it catches up with him—it always catches up with you, he knows—and his head is symphonic with it, his stomach undulating with feedback. It undoes him. He is afloat, not of this world. He needs an anchor, and he finds it in the Stroker's beautiful, sad eyes.

A small rivulet of blood—or two of them, because everything is double—drips down her temple and onto her cheek. It looks like a teardrop, and for a second Nathaniel thinks she is crying for him.

Only Nathaniel knows that can't be. Tears are not blood-colored, and no one cries for him. Still, he is riveted by the trail the bloody tear tracks down her cheek. It is the prettiest of flowers, the loveliest of scars. He reaches out to touch her cheek. And though everything is tilted and blurry and double, he does not miss, and though she is beautiful and a stranger, she does not recoil.

— — —

No, Freya does not recoil, but her insides undulate too. *No one touches me like that anymore,* she thinks. Which is a strange thing to think, because these days she's touched all the time, by stylists and trainers, by her mother, by a series of doctors, by Hayden and the execs from the label, who let their hands linger on her shoulders, her legs, her waist, just a moment longer than is comfortable. All these people who are there for her, to help her, their touch feels dead, but this stranger's touch just made her heart trip.

What the fuck?

— — —

The blood from her cheek is on Nathaniel's finger. He does not know what to do with it. Wipe it? Lick it? Transfuse it?

"Hey, you," the Stroker calls. "You think you might give us a hand over here?"

The "you" in question approaches and begins to snap right in front of Nathaniel's eyes.

This is extremely unpleasant.

"I'm not sure that's necessary," she says. "He's awake."

The snapping continues. "Are you okay?" the Snapper asks.

You're doing okay, aren't you? People used to ask Nathaniel that sometimes—the teammates he practiced with, the girls who used to flutter around him, the coaches who thought he had promise. *You're doing okay?* they asked. After Mom left. After Grandma Mary died. After he lost his eye. *You're all right, aren't you?*

(Just us, buddy.)

Later, Nathaniel figured out it wasn't really a question. People wanted reassurances; they wanted to be let off the hook, so even though he wasn't all right or okay, even though he was a frog boiling in a pot, even though he was being swallowed up by the ground beneath him, he answered: "It's all good."

Which is such an obvious lie. When are things ever *all* good?

But people eat it up. When he tells them it's all good, they smile. Their relief is always palpable and always heartbreaking, because Nathaniel has once again allowed himself to think they meant it this time. He's like Charlie Brown with that stupid football.

If you need anything, just holler, they say, reciting lines in a script. To which Nathaniel answers, on cue, *You bet.* And it hurts worse for allowing himself to hope.

Nope. He's not falling for that again. He's not winding up flat on his back. He's already flat on his back.

He starts to stand up.

"Help him up," the Stroker demands, and she takes one hand, the Snapper taking the other.

Give me your hand, Nat, his dad used to say as he taught him to climb trees, higher and higher, above the canopy, where he claimed you could see all the way to Canada. His mom would get so angry. "I don't know who's the bigger child."

He's steadier now. He's fine.

(Not fine, not really, but upright.)

He just needs a moment here, to gather his wits, to gain his bearings, to have his hands held by two strangers before they let go.

"Are you okay?" the Snapper asks again.

"It's all . . ." he begins to tell them, to release them of culpability. And before he can finish the sentence, before he can say the word *good*, he throws up. Right onto the Stroker's feet.

— — —

Freya stares at her feet. Soiled with vomit. She has a short fuse these days. Anything sets her off: traffic lights taking too long, the weather report being off by three degrees, anything anyone says to her.

Some random stranger just puked on her feet.

And she feels like crying, but not because she's annoyed or grossed out.

What the fuck?

She excuses herself to clean her feet.

— — —

That Harun is a coward is not up for debate.

When he saw the girl fall from the bridge onto the boy below, what was his first impulse? Was it to run to their aid? To call an ambulance? To get help?

No, it was to flee.

Again, to restate: his cowardice is not up for debate.

The reason Harun wanted to run, initially, was that he had this terrible feeling that the accident was his fault. Moments before, he had been essentially cursing both of those people for not being James. Even if he had not asked for it in so many words, he had asked for it in intention—which is, he knows, what God listens to. People lie all the time about what they want, but intentions are pure.

So at first, he had stood by and tried to think of the appropriate prayer to say when you accidentally ask God to do something bad to other people. *As'alu Allah al 'azim rabbil 'arshil 'azim an yashifika* was all he came up with, asking Allah to cure them. (He's given up asking that for himself.)

But he would like the record to show, when he saw the heap of bodies, imagining them both dead, or at the very least gravely injured by his thoughts, he snapped himself out of his fugue state and walked closer, planning to Do the Right Thing—administer CPR, call 911, say the correct prayer.

But at that particular point, the bodies disentangled and the young female portion of the heap sat up. He was close, close enough to see her face: the sharp cheekbones, the prominent oval eyes, the regal neck. And then she'd asked him for his help. With that voice.

"One day, we'll meet her," James used to say as they huddled around his phone, watching one of her videos. "We'll tell her how we're her first, biggest fans. She'll be famous, bigger than Beyoncé, but we'll be best friends. She'll sing at our wedding."

Statements like that took Harun's breath away. It seemed daring enough for him to imagine a future with James, let alone things like a wedding, let alone a wedding where James's favorite singer, whom they'd never met, would sing.

Now, as he watches her throw away her shoes and rinse

her feet with a bottle of Poland Spring, he has three thoughts.

The first is: *It can't be her.* There is simply no way. Not this person, in this park, on this day. He is conjuring her as a way to bring back James.

His second thought: *James, whose last words to me were* Get the fuck out my life.

His third thought: *If it is her, James will have to forgive me.*

The young man he's holding heaves against Harun, and Harun turns his glance away from her to him. Him, he now sees, is very good-looking, the kind of pretty white boy James called a "confection."

"I'm all good," the confection keeps saying, even as he sways like a green tree in a strong gale.

She (he can't bring himself to even think her name) returns, barefoot, and takes hold of her half of the swaying tree of a confection. Harun can't look at her face, so he stares at her feet. Which are still wet.

"Thanks for your help," she says in that husky voice of hers.

"Uhh," says Harun.

"It's all good," the swaying tree of a confection says.

It doesn't look all good to Harun. Aside from the swaying, there's the eyes. Two different colors. Can a fall do that?

"Is there someone we can call?" she asks.

James, thinks Harun. But no, this isn't about him. He turns to the swaying tree, who is squinting as if someone just asked him the square root of 17,432.

"Dad?" Nathaniel says at last.

"Dad. So your father's here?" she asks.

Nathaniel sways and nods.

"Do you have a way to contact him?"

Harun sees the phone on the path, alongside the other spilled contents of his backpack. He scrambles to pick it up. "Perhaps you can call?"

The swaying tree opens the phone, one of those ancient flip numbers, and presses a button. It rings loudly enough for them all to hear. The voicemail picks up. A man's voice: "Tell me something good."

The command irks Harun. What if there's nothing good to tell? What then?

There's a long beep, followed by a robotic voice that informs them the voicemail box is full, and Harun understands he must be in the minority, that lots of people have had so many good things to share that the voicemail box is full of glad tidings.

"I think we should probably get you to a hospital, Nathaniel," she says, turning to Harun. "He seems pretty out of it."

Well, a human being did fall on him. And even though that human is *her* (he's almost certain), it must have hurt. Harun suspects the boy is concussed. Abdullah got hit with a cricket bat once and could not remember their address or his birth date.

"What do you think?" she asks.

It takes Harun a moment to realize *she* is asking him for his opinion. He responds, helpfully, with another "Uhhh . . ."

"Do you think you could see if there's one nearby?"

"Yes, yes, hospital, hospital," Harun says, his speech returning to him in double. He pulls out his phone, enormously relieved to have a focus for his attention that is not *her*. But his thumb has a mind of its own, because it's hovering over the text app, so tempted to tell James whom he is with, to snap a surreptitious picture. Surely, if James knew, he would relent. He would take him back.

"Did you find one?" she asks, and Harun feels his ears go red because this poor boy is clearly unwell and he is still thinking about James. Will he ever not be? Amir has promised him yes, that one day he will look back and not believe this happened. It will be wiped from the record.

He prays so.

He prays not.

She clears her throat.

He scuttles to the map, finds an urgent care clinic. "Yes, yes. There's one on Columbus Avenue. It says it's about a quarter mile from here by foot."

"Can you walk that far?" she asks Nathaniel. "If we help you?"

"We?" Harun blurts out in joy and relief and realizes, too late, that it sounds as if he is objecting to helping when it's the *we* that has tripped him up. "Yes, yes. Of course, of course. We will. We will."

"Really, you don't have to," Nathaniel says. "It's all good."

"I'm sure it is, but let's get you checked out by a doctor," she says. She bends down to pick up the rest of the contents of his backpack, as if she were a normal human being and not *her*.

Harun should help—he is merely an ordinary person—but seeing the boxers, the books, the T-shirts makes him flash on the suitcase that Ammi has lovingly packed for him, full of new clothes, a new *kurta*, gifts. And when he does, he is paralyzed by shame. And here he had thought he had plumbed the depths of his shame when, on the edge of this very park, James told him to get the fuck out of his life.

"Okay," she says, hoisting the backpack onto her shoulder. "Let's go."

"Really, you don't have to," Nathaniel says. "I'm meeting my dad later. It's all good."

"Stop saying that!" Harun is surprised and also abashed by the harshness of his tone. He has no reason to be angry with this boy, who may not be James but who was just walking through the park, minding his own business, when he was fallen on top of. It's not his fault if James asked Harun to believe that even if it wasn't all good, it might be, when Harun knows, has always known, it wasn't, it couldn't be.

It's the hoping that makes it hurt.

Harun knows that.

— — —

Nathaniel knows that.

— — —

Freya knows it too.

— — —

If she's perfectly honest, Freya can admit that her intentions are not completely honorable either. Now that the fog has cleared and she realizes what she's done—fallen off the bridge while staring at images of her happy sister, who said yes, onto some guy below—her concern is less for his well-being than her own.

She sees the situation through her mother's eyes—"He could sue us"—and Hayden's eyes—"the wrong kind of publicity"—and though she generally finds her mother in particular to be not just preemptively paranoid about people wanting to sue Freya, but aspirationally so (*dream it, be it*), Freya is properly assessing the situation.

She fell off a bridge, onto an innocent bystander. Some other guy watched the whole thing. He has a phone in his hand. For all she knows, he has the entire thing on video and is just waiting to email the photos to some gossip website or post them on Twitter. How many hits would that get? The one thing people love more than witnessing a success is watching a downfall.

The guy she fell on doesn't seem to recognize her (he doesn't seem to recognize himself), but the Lurker does. Back when Freya was getting big enough to start getting negative comments, she sometimes engaged with the haters. *Hey, I'm only human*, she might say. Or: *That hurt*. And it was crazy because sometimes they backed down. It's been a while since she's done that. Hayden has told her not to respond to the fans so directly anymore. Not even to look at what they're saying about her. "That's my job now," he's said.

Still, the best way to defang someone is to kill them with kindness. Which is why she corralled the Lurker into helping get the guy, Nathaniel, to urgent care.

(It's prudence, is all. It has nothing to do with the way her stomach flipped when Nathaniel touched her face.)

By the time they reach the urgent care clinic, Freya's feet are black and her mood even darker. She realizes she has just roped herself into something stupid, yoked herself to these two people who could do her harm. She should've called the publicist, but she's not sure she'll take her calls anymore.

"What seems to be the issue?" the receptionist at the urgent care asks.

"We were in the park," the Lurker explains, "and she fell off a bridge onto him and knocked him out."

She can picture how this would all play out in the court of social media.

On her phone. Navel-gazing. Typical!

Used to like her, but she got 2 full of herself.

Truth.

Such a bitch.

U no she thru her sister under a 🚐.

The receptionist, with the bored expression of someone who has heard this particular story a dozen times today alone, hands them a clipboard with a sheaf of paperwork. "Fill this out, and I'll need the insurance card."

Freya turns to Nathaniel, who has not said more than two words aside from emptily reassuring them that it was all good, and she wonders if he's brain damaged.

He was a brilliant mathematician, they would say. *On the verge of curing cancer. Until she fell on him.*

Another life ruined.

Hate that bitch.

"Insurance card," the receptionist repeats. "Otherwise, I need payment up front for the appointment."

"Do you have an insurance card?" Freya asks him. But the question does not seem to register at all. "Can I see your wallet?"

He hands it to her, and she rifles through. There's the driver's license, a bit of cash, the boarding pass, some business card, and, tucked into the torn lining, a creased photo strip. She peers at the picture of what is almost certainly a much younger Nathaniel and an older man who previews what Nathaniel might look like in another ten years—maybe his father? She feels a tug from deep inside, as if there were an invisible cord looped around the area where her heart should be.

She reaches into her wallet and pulls out her own credit card. She can hear her mother, Hayden, the publicists tell her that she has just provided a paper trail of her guilt. *But I was just trying to do the right thing,* she tells her invisible judges.

What do you know about the right thing?

Freya's plan had been to get him here to an urgent care clinic and be on her dreary way, but now, hearing the invisible critics corner her (*You paid for him because you were responsible*), she cannot get away so easily. Sighing heavily, she leads Nathaniel to the seats and hands him the forms. The Lurker is still there. Maybe she can get him to leave his phone lying around so she can delete whatever pictures he took before they wind up a headline in the *Post*: *Diva Ditches KO'd Pedestrian*.

Who's she kidding? She can't sing, and if she can't sing there won't be fame, let alone celebrity or even buzz, and certainly no gossip items in the *Post*. The fans will disappear. And then . . .

She blinks hard, trying to dislodge the thought, and turns to Nathaniel, who's staring at the clipboard as though it were written in hieroglyphics. At this rate, they're going to be here all day. She snatches the clipboard away from him. "How about I fill that out for you?" she says, trying her best not to let her impatience seep through.

He nods.

The name she knows: Nathaniel Haley. "Address? Date of birth?"

"I don't have one," he says, and Freya thinks that he really is addled. He's still holding his wallet, so she takes it back and removes his driver's license, copying the pertinent info from there. Six foot two. Brown hair, green eyes. Nineteen years old. The address is just a state route in Washington, but when she writes it down, she pictures a house on the edge of a forest. She hears birds singing.

"Emergency contact?" she asks.

His face goes blank.

She fishes out the business card and reads the name: Hector Fuentes. Is that the man in the photo strip? "Hector Fuentes? Is that your father?" she asks, though Nathaniel doesn't look like the kind of person who has a father named Hector Fuentes, but then again, Freya doesn't look like the kind of person who has a mother named Nancy Greenberg.

Nathaniel hesitates for a moment, shakes his head.

"Can you tell me your father's phone number?"

When he returns a blank look, she doesn't blame him. Who remembers phone numbers anymore? She can get it off that ancient flip phone he used to call his father in the park, but she's not sure how those phones work, so even though it implicates her further, she writes down her own number.

— — —

Harun listens to Freya quiz Nathaniel about allergies (shrimp). He feels left out. He wishes he had an allergy to offer. But he's not allergic to anything, except perhaps himself. This is a thing. He looked it up once. It can be fatal.

"Have you had any of the following?" Freya—he's sure it's her now, he saw the credit card—lists a number of medical conditions. They include ailments like tuberculosis, arrhythmia, and emphysema, and Harun can't help but notice that the most common maladies, the ones that will really hurt a person—corrosive shame, shattered heart, betrayed family—are not included.

She finishes the forms and turns them in. Harun knows that whatever use he might have had is expired, but she is his last chance at getting James back. What are the odds of them meeting, on this of all days? He must find a way to extend his usefulness.

The nurse calls Nathaniel's name.

Freya says, "You'll be okay?"

Nathaniel begins to answer, but Harun interrupts. "We should go with him. To talk to the doctor."

Freya looks extremely unhappy about this, but, sighing, she stands and reluctantly follows.

— — —

They all three squeeze into the examination room, where, after the nurse takes Nathaniel's vital signs, it becomes apparent that they are complete strangers with nothing in common and nothing to say to one another.

Awkward silence ensues as they each attempt to find some place in the small room to look that is not at one another.

Freya takes out her phone. The screen, she now sees, is cracked from the fall in the park, frozen on the image of her sister—*she said yes!*—with her stupid fiancé. The Lurker has his phone in his hand. Is he tweeting about her? Has he already posted pictures? She should check. She should tell someone. But she can't bear it. She doesn't want to know. She shuts off her screen but pretends to be busy on her phone so she can take a moment to surreptitiously size up her new companions.

The Lurker is jittery, big brown eyes popping out of brown skin a shade or two darker than hers. He exudes a sort of nervous energy that makes him look like a frightened animal and takes away from the fact that under all those jangling nerves is a cute guy, moderately well-dressed, trying desperately to play it cool.

The other one, Nathaniel, looks like the sort of person who's never played it cool in his life. Looking like that, he wouldn't need to. He's the sort of attractive—tall and lanky and possessing bone structure people pay money for—that others need to play it cool around. Though not Freya. She has been inundated with beauty so much that she's no longer impressed by it. She would be unimpressed by Nathaniel too were it not for the mismatched eyes, one green, one grayish. They mar his perfection. They make him breathtaking.

"You're pretty enough," Hayden told her once, "but it's your voice that makes you distinctive." It follows that without a voice she is indistinctive. She is nobody.

There's a hard knock at the door as the doctor comes in. Freya scopes him out straightaway: young and toothily handsome but with a smug smile that wrecks everything.

"What seems to be the problem?" he asks.

It's the same opening the doctor used earlier that day. Why do they ask that? Can't they just read the forms? Only this time there is no Freya's mother to step into the maw with the explanation, and Nathaniel remains mute.

"We were in the park," Freya begins. "And I sort of fell off a bridge, onto Nathaniel."

"You fell off a bridge? Did you faint?"

"No," Freya says. She wonders if she should've said she

did faint, because this would make her seem less culpable. *Not her fault,* they would tweet. *She fell after fainting. Poor thing. Lost her voice, you know.* "I just lost my balance."

He wheels his stool in Freya's direction, stopping just short of her bare feet.

"Whoa!" he says, as if he just noticed her feet had been amputated and she was walking on bloody nubs. "What happened?"

"To my feet? They just got dirty," Freya says.

"How?" he asks.

"From dirt," the Lurker mutters under his breath, and Freya almost smiles.

The doctor turns toward the Lurker. "Are you the one she fell on?"

"No," he answers. "I'm Harun. I am a bystander."

"A Samaritan, really. Harun helped me get Nathaniel here," Freya says, relieved to have learned Harun's name in such a non-awkward way. She was taught always to use people's names. It makes them feel important. If she uses his name, maybe he won't turn the internet against her.

"Who's Nathaniel?" the doctor asks.

She points to the corner, where, for someone as tall as Nathaniel is, he's doing a pretty good job of disappearing.

The doctor finally tears his gaze away from Freya and looks at the chart. "Nathaniel Haley," he reads.

"Yeah," Nathaniel says in a voice as wispy as fog.

"So you were fallen on by this one?" He gestures to Freya.

"Yeah, I guess," he says.

"Not the worst way to get knocked out," the doctor says, aiming a conspiratorial glance in Freya's direction. She looks down, thinking: *Stop. Just stop.*

"It factor," Hayden had called it. "Y'know, that invisible thing some people got that makes others wanna get closer. You can't fake it. You either got it or you don't." Freya had it, Hayden said. Sabrina did not, Hayden said.

"And you blacked out?" the doctor asks.

Nathaniel shrugs.

"Yes, he did," Freya replies.

"I need to hear it from the patient."

Nathaniel doesn't answer. Freya begins to wonder if he really is brain damaged.

"Yes," Harun says. "He did. She fell onto him. He blacked out."

"I'd appreciate it," the doctor says in an unpleasant tone, "if you allowed me to interview the patient."

"But how can he tell you what happened when it happened to him?" Harun says. "I was there. I saw."

— — —

I saw.

Harun has no way of knowing at this moment that these words are more healing to Nathaniel than anything the doctor might do. Someone saw.

"So you lost consciousness?" the doctor asks Nathaniel again.

Nathaniel looks at Freya, at Harun, who both nod.

"Yes," he says.

"And he vomited," Harun adds. "On her shoes."

"So that's why you're barefoot!" the doctor says to Freya. "You shouldn't walk through the city like that. I'll see if we can get you some shoes from the lost and found."

"I'll be fine," she says.

"You might step on glass."

"No, really. It's all good," she says, glancing at Nathaniel with a look, like it's a private joke she's tossing at him. But he doesn't catch it. (He used to be a really good catcher, back when he played first base.) Not because he cannot but because he dares not.

This has already gone way too far. There's really no need for this.

But the doctor has pulled out a penlight and is examining Nathaniel's eyes.

"Heterochromia," he declares.

"Is that like a hematoma?" Harun asks.

"No. It's when you have different-colored eyes. Though the left pupil here is really fixed."

"You mean the pupil in my prosthetic eye?" Nathaniel asks.

"Right. Of course. You threw me with the different colors. But I like it. Is it a kind of David Bowie homage?"

"Can we get on with the exam?" Freya asks impatiently. "We don't have all day."

The doctor rolls his stool over to the computer. "Okay, Nate. I'm going to ask about symptoms, and you answer on a scale of zero to six, zero being not a problem, three being moderate, six being severe. Got it?"

"I think so," Nathaniel replies.

"Headache?"

"Yes."

"Zero to six?"

It's a four, but he doesn't want anyone to worry. "Maybe a two."

"Pressure in the head?"

"Yeah. Maybe three."

"Blurred vision?"

"It's all good now."

"A number."

"Zero, maybe one."

The doctor goes through the list: neck pain, balance problems. Nathaniel answers in a monotone: two, three, two.

"How about sadness?" the doctor asks.

"Sadness?"

"Yeah, sadness."

"You want me to rate sadness?"

"Yep," the doctor says. "Zero to six, please, Nate."

— — —

Freya is over it. Over doctors who pretend to know everything, who act like they can fix her, who ask what's wrong without reading a chart, who ask people to sing "Happy Birthday" or to measure sadness on a scale of zero to six.

"His name is Nathaniel!" she snarls with an irritated confidence she has no right to. For all she knows, he goes by Nate.

— — —

He does not. Though his father calls him Nat.

— — —

"And what does it have to do with a concussion?" Harun asks. Is this doctor even a doctor? He scans the walls for a medical school diploma.

"Hey, I don't write the checklist," the doctor says, fully out of patience. "So how about you give me a number so I can get you out of here. Sadness, zero to six?"

"No, he can't give you a number," Harun says.

"You can't measure sadness in numbers," Freya agrees.

"So how would you measure it?" the doctor asks. "Please do tell, so I can refer it to the American Academy of Neurology."

— — —

The question is asked in a most scathingly sarcastic tone, but Freya, Harun, and Nathaniel all ponder it seriously.

— — —

Freya thinks of music, and then silence, and being totally alone.

— — —

Harun thinks of love, and family, and *Get the fuck out my life.*

— — —

Nathaniel thinks of his father, and Sam and Frodo, and a house being swallowed up by the forest.

— — —

They may be complete strangers, with different lives and different problems, but there in that examination room they are measuring sadness the same way. They are measuring it in loss.

THE ORDER OF LOSS
PART IV

NATHANIEL

"Nat, you gotta come see this," Dad called the minute I walked in the door.

I took a breath and pushed back against the irritation. I was sweaty from baseball practice, and I needed to shower and do Dad's breakfast and lunch dishes and get dinner going, and I needed to go online to register for a free SAT prep course.

The day before, my mother had called me, wanting to know if I'd started thinking about college. "You're going to be a junior. Has your father even started this process?"

I assured her he had, fumbling some lie about arranging to visit schools together, which is something I knew a couple of kids had done with their parents. Mom didn't press. The woman who'd once said she couldn't live with two children now had two new children and her hands were full, so I knew she wouldn't follow up. Still, I'd made an appointment with a guidance counselor and had seen her earlier that day.

"Nat, hurry up!" Dad called from the living room.

Sometimes if I ignored him, he got distracted. Most of the time, he only got more insistent, and it became that much harder to calm him down. It was better to see what had gotten him all riled up, talk to him a bit, and maybe I could get on the computer.

The guidance counselor had been surprised I hadn't been to see her before. "Your grades are pretty good, and a sophomore on the varsity baseball team is very impressive," she said. We'd made it all the way to the division finals and we'd had a few scouts come to our games. "With your grades, you could get into a fine school," she'd said. "Maybe even a partial scholarship if you play baseball. Not a division one school, but somewhere smaller—if you do well on the SATs. Let's get you set up for a course."

"Nat!"

I went into the living room. The TV was on, as it usually was since Dad had stopped working. I'd learned to gauge his mood not from how he was acting but from what he was watching. Cartoons, CNN, *Real Housewives* meant he was checked out. Documentaries meant he was good. Dad loved documentaries, not because of what they told you but because of what they suggested.

I squinted at the TV. Some guy was riding a bicycle.

"Yeah?" I said.

"The guy riding the bike is blind." Dad smiled triumphantly. But I knew there was more. There was always more. "Hear that sound?"

It was faint but unmistakable, like a woodpecker.

"He's clicking," Dad said. "Like a bat."

"Echo-locating," I said.

Dad snapped his fingers. "Exactly! He's been doing that since he was little, when he lost both his eyes to cancer. He does not have eyes, but he can see—literally see."

"You can't *literally* see if you don't have eyes."

"Can't you?" Dad asked with that glimmer in his own eyes, and I sighed because I knew what that meant.

"It got me thinking," Dad continued. And then he was off to the races, his latest theory he wanted to try out. If a blind man could see with other parts of his brain, what else might we be able to do? "We put up roadblocks in our mind that limit us. But we can remove those blocks too. What was it William Blake said? 'If the doors of perception were cleansed, everything would appear to man as it is, infinite.'"

His speech started to pick up speed, as it did when he really went on a tear. Soon he would be breathless, the thoughts coming too fast for him to keep up. "Do you see? Do you see?" he asked. "What if we could unlock, if we could just set our minds free?" He stopped to knock himself on his temple, not softly, to make a point, but with intensity, like he wanted to punch his brain.

I gently grabbed his hand and held it in my lap until he calmed down.

"Don't you see?" Dad's voice was a reverent whisper. "What it means is that the only limitation on how we live our lives is up here." His touched my temple this time, gently. He reached for two strips of heavy cotton, cut, I saw, from one of the few sets of intact bedsheets we still had.

"Let's go into the forest," Dad said. "Let's go see if we can't expand our consciousness."

I didn't want to expand anything. I had homework to do. An SAT prep course to register for. The day's dishes were still sitting on the table, and dinner needed to be started. But I knew if I didn't go, Dad would go without me.

He wanted to walk deep into the woods, but I managed to steer him toward a clearing not that far away, a place clear of obstacles, cliffs, large boulders. It was where, four years earlier, we had scattered Grandma Mary's ashes.

"I'll do you first," Dad said.

"Okay." I had no intention of staying blindfolded, of echo-locating. I was here to make sure Dad didn't fall off a cliff.

I let Dad put the blindfold on me. He tied it tight, and the darkness was sudden and absolute. I carefully sat down on a fallen log, so Dad, who wasn't dumb, would think I was participating in this activity and not just humoring him.

At first, I felt the familiar, itchy crawl of impatience. How long would this go on? But as I sat there in the darkness, something strange began to happen. It was like someone turned up the volume of the forest. I could hear the sound of a leaf falling to the earth, of it degrading to mulch. I could hear the beavers pushing stones into the river. And then I was hearing past the forest. In the darkness, I heard a bell ringing in a far-off church. I heard an airplane flying at forty thousand feet. I heard the sound of a girl singing. And then the other senses kicked in. I smelled dates, as if the seeds Grandma Mary and I had planted had borne fruit. I tasted flavors I could not describe.

That was the maddening thing about my father. Just when you wanted to write him off as a nut job or a Peter Pan, he would make you go traipsing blindfolded through the forest and you would touch the hem of something mysterious.

"God damn it!" Dad yelped. "Shit!"

I yanked off my mask and light returned, and the secrets the forest had been ready to tell quieted themselves.

There was Dad, clicking wildly, flailing his hands, teetering toward a ditch.

"Dad!" I took off running. "Dad, wait!" I caught up with him a few feet before the ravine, but he kept going, wildly windmilling his arms around. "Dad, stop!" I reached out to yank him back, but he jerked forward, snapping a green tree branch that ricocheted back with the force of a whip.

I didn't feel pain. It was only when I felt the blood, warm and trickling down my cheek, that I knew something had happened.

"Dad," I called. "I think I'm hurt."

He didn't turn around. "You're fine," he said.

The blood was running into my mouth now, the vision in my left eye going murky.

"I'm bleeding."

"If a blind man can see, you can handle a little blood."

It was more than a little, but I knew when he was too far gone.

"Put some leaves on it," Dad said. "Who knows? Maybe they'll have antibacterial properties like the tree frog." He'd watched a documentary about that years ago.

"Dad!"

"You can't discover things if you don't take risks. You'll be fine."

"Dad."

"Imagine if Frodo and Sam gave up every time they hit a hiccup. Imagine that."

I knew better than to argue with him when he got like this. My choice was either to go back home and take care of it or to wait out here with him.

I waited out there in the woods for at least another hour, as my father expanded his consciousness and I bled into soggy leaves. By the time we got back to the house, my eye had swollen shut. I went into the bathroom and cleaned up the cut as best I could.

When I came out, Dad was in the kitchen, cleaning up the dishes and running the garbage disposal, something he never did.

"That was life-changing, wasn't it?" he said. He glanced at me, finally noticing the wound. "You should put some ice on that."

Except there was no ice in the freezer, and it was late and I had to start dinner. So I put a washcloth on it, figuring it would get better. It had stopped hurting and was beginning to itch.

I stayed home from school the next day because I'd slept badly and I looked awful. The eye was puffy and swollen shut. I briefly thought about going to the doctor, except we didn't have a doctor aside from the one Dad went to at the free clinic in town to get his meds. I thought of going to the ER but worried about how much it would cost and what would happen if it got back to Mom. I was getting too old for custody battles, but I couldn't be too careful.

Dad stayed locked in his room, scribbling in his notebooks. He would be like this until the fever broke, and then he'd be on to the next documentary—about serial killers, about mountain gorillas, about salt, about suicide tourism—that would click an idea in his brain and send him running again.

When I woke up the following morning, my eye was on fire, an ooze of bloody pus trickling down my cheek. I went to the nurse's office at school and was immediately sent to the ER, and it was there that the doctors said the entire socket was infected and the eyeball itself had been deprived of blood for so long the tissue was probably dead. The eyeball would likely have to be removed.

The surgery was delayed because we needed parental consent and Dad was not answering his phone. I made up a story about how he was a writer and turned off his phone when he was working. It wasn't that far from the truth.

"What about your mother?" they asked me.

My mother could not find out about this. I'd see to that just as I'd made sure she'd never found out about the week we'd gone without electricity or the time Dad had left me in the forest all night.

(*Don't tell your mother.*)

"My mom's dead," I told the doctors.

They eventually got hold of Dad and I was rushed into surgery. I woke up alone, in a dark room, and knew my eye was gone. As I lay there, groggy, my head throbbing, I wanted someone to wrap their arms around me, to kiss my forehead, to tell me things would be okay. But nobody did. Tentatively, I touched the gauze packing around my eye, and realized, with equal parts terror and relief, this secret would be impossible to conceal from my mother. Because she would see, and she would know, and if she knew, she wouldn't let me stay here. Would she?

My father came into the room, and when he saw me awake, he began to weep. "Oh, Nat. Oh, buddy," he said. "Look at you."

At the sight of my father doubled over, sobbing, I understood that I would not tell my mother. The decision had already been made long ago. And with that, the lie I'd told the doctors about her being dead suddenly became true. To keep this secret from her, I'd have to keep myself from her. The realization sent a bolt of fury through me, shaking off the remaining sedation. In that terrible, tiny moment, I didn't just hate my father, I wished he were dead.

But the moment passed, leaving me exhausted, and hungover with shame. I didn't hate my father. I loved him and he loved me.

He had begun sobbing convulsively, like he'd heard my horrible thoughts. I knew if I didn't calm him down, it would only get worse. So I told him what I'd already learned people wanted to hear: "It's all good."

"But you lost your eye," he said.

"It couldn't be saved," the doctors had told me. So I saved the only thing I still could. Or I tried to.

"Maybe I had to lose the eye to gain sight," I told him.

The look on his face, it was so hopeful it was painful. "Really? You really think so?"

I didn't think so. I didn't believe half of what my dad said anymore, but I couldn't write him off completely. Because he was occasionally right. And because he was Dad. And we were a fellowship of two.

"Really," I told him.

THE ORDER OF LOSS
PART V

FREYA

The first video really was an accident. People didn't believe that. They thought it was part of the concocted narrative, but it was the one detail of all of this that Hayden didn't invent. It just happened.

Sabrina had been right. Two years later, our father was still gone. The promises to come back, to have us visit him, turned out to be made of smoke. The weekly Skype calls had begun to dwindle, and on the phone he was vague about his life. He no longer asked if I wanted to visit. He no longer asked me if I sang.

But I did still sing—only with Sabrina now. Every day. After school, Sabrina made the snacks—grilled cheese sandwiches with sliced tomatoes—and helped me with my homework. She was a far better student than me, straight As across the board. When homework was finished, we listened to music together, picking apart songs we loved, seeing if we could sing them better.

Sometimes we went online, watched videos on YouTube.

Other times, we went on Facebook, trying to get a glimpse of our father. Back when he lived here it had been his professional page, with videos of him playing gigs or offering music lessons after Mom had come up with the idea that he should teach to earn some money. These days the posts showed him at church, at family meals, smiling broadly, arms around aunts and uncles and cousins we'd never met. Did he miss us? I couldn't tell. The status updates were usually in Amharic.

That day, we were scrolling through Facebook when we came upon a picture of a woman holding a baby bundled in a green blanket. The caption read: በመጨረሻ ወንድ ልጅ አለን.

"Let's look it up," Sabrina said, and we pasted the words into a translation program. I thought it would say something about a new nephew, a new cousin for me, but the translator spat out: *Finally, we have a son.* And suddenly I understood why the phone calls had dwindled.

I began to cry, something I did often, which irritated Sabrina, who never cried. But this time, she patted me on the shoulder. "I'm sorry," she said.

Her pity made me cry harder. She looked at the screen. "Solomon doesn't deserve your tears." Solomon, not Dad. "I mean, how could he forget you like this?"

You. As if it only affected me.

"You know what you should do? You should post a song or something. Show him how amazing you are. What he's lost."

Sing what you can't say, my father had said. That was what Billie and Nina and Josephine and Gigi did.

"Okay."

"Let's clean you up first."

Sabrina mopped my face with a washcloth and carefully did my makeup. "Do you know what you want to sing?" she asked.

Yes. I wanted to sing "Tschay Hailu," the lullaby my father had sung to me and that he would now be singing to his new son. I fetched an empty trash can for accompaniment, and Sabrina hit RECORD.

My intention had been to send a greeting to my new brother, a reminder to my father, but when I started singing, something else came out, something primal and aching and pure. I kept singing, drumming even harder, and my voice went places it had never been before.

When it was over, I felt better, just like the night when Sabrina first sang with me. I didn't even want to post it. Singing the song was enough.

"Oh, we're definitely posting it." Sabrina uploaded the video onto her Facebook page.

"Huh," Sabrina said the next day when we checked on the post. She'd tagged our father, so the video had shown on his page, but he must've untagged himself, because it was no longer there.

But on her own page, we saw that the video had been shared sixty-seven times. It had garnered more than a hundred comments, some from Sabrina's friends but others from people I didn't know. I was devastated that my father had untagged himself. Why would he do that? Was he embarrassed about us? Ashamed that he'd left us? Did he not like the video?

The only thing that eased my pain was all the comments. Later, when Mom came home and Sabrina was helping her with dinner, I read them all. Twice over. They were so nice. And they filled the hole my father's silence had left.

I took a copy of the video and edited it down and posted it on Twitter.

By the next day, the video had hundreds of shares, thousands of likes, and so many more comments. I read them all. And read them again. They made me feel so good.

I showed Sabrina. "Why'd you post it again?" she asked. "Solomon probably doesn't have Twitter, and he already saw it on Facebook."

"Look at how many people shared it, though."

Sabrina looked. She seemed unimpressed.

"Maybe we should show Mom?"

"Yeah," she said. "I'm sure she'll love that you sent our father a song."

"But it's weird that it got so many shares." I tried to sound casual. "It kind of went viral. We should tell her before she finds out from someone else."

Sabrina sighed. "Fine. I'll show her."

— — —

"Huh," Mom said. "I've been reading about how the internet is creating a new kind of star. There's potential for actual money."

"How?" Sabrina asked.

"I'm not sure," our mother said. "Let's post another one. Why don't you do it together this time? You girls sing so beautifully. What do you think, Sabrina?"

Even back then, there must have been a small acorn in my heart. Because I felt it, nubby and shriveled and shouting, *What about me?* when Mom said that. *I* was the one born singing. *I* was the one who'd gotten all those likes from my video. But no one asked me.

"Okay," Sabrina said. "Why not?"

— — —

The first few videos were duds. But Mom, under the thrall of *The Path*, was convinced if she dreamed it hard enough, it would happen. She began reading up on what made successful videos. She determined that we needed a hook, a look, and a sound.

The sound was mostly dictated by covers. We hadn't started writing our own material yet. The look was my doing: I wanted us to look like Billie and Josephine and Gigi. And the hook was that we were sisters who looked nothing like sisters.

"What should we call you?" Mom asked. "The Kebede Sisters?"

Sabrina wrinkled her nose. "The Sisters Kebede," she tried. She shook her head. "Sounds weird." She paused, tapping her fingers against her chin. "What about the Sisters K?"

"The Sisters K," Mom said. "I like that."

— — —

By the time we were summoned to Hayden Booth's offices four years later, the Sisters K had a YouTube channel (220,000 subscribers), an Instagram feed (780,000 followers), a Twitter account (375,000 followers), an official Facebook page and several fan pages, and a SoundCloud channel with more than twenty original songs.

We also had a manager: Mom. She watched other people's successful videos obsessively, trying to figure out what worked and what didn't. She mapped out weekly schedules, analyzed web traffic to determine when we should post. She stayed up late into the night, monitoring the comments and shares. When our videos earned the first bit of advertising money, she used it to hire a consultant to help us hone our look and leverage—or, as she said, "monetize"—our growing popularity.

"It's interesting," the publicist said, going through some of the comments. "They seem personally invested in Freya."

"Probably because she responds to all of their comments," Sabrina said dismissively. "Every. Single. One."

I blushed and looked down, embarrassed and ashamed. Because Sabrina was right. I did read every comment and I responded, in the early days, to nearly all of them. It was the only thing that made me feel like I was part of this.

Though we called ourselves the Sisters K, it was really the Mom and Sabrina show. Sabrina and I might have sung together, and we sometimes wrote songs together, but she and Mom discussed every aspect of the business, and she went to Mom with every new song we wrote. They conspired. They plotted. And our family went back to being a three-legged chair.

The comments, however, were all mine. When I started replying to fans, they began addressing me directly. While Mom and Sabrina sat in front of one computer, analyzing engagements, talking about me, I could quietly open my phone and really engage, knowing someone would be there for me.

"Actually," the publicist told us, "that's a really smart strategy. It makes the fans feel like they're a part of your success. Those kinds of superfans are the ones that'll take you from a novelty act to the next level."

"Wonderful!" Mom said. "Freya, keep doing what you're doing. Sabrina and I will keep up on our end."

— — —

We began to earn more advertising money from our videos. Mom went from full-time to part-time at her job as a hospital administrator. She read articles about the highest-paid internet celebrities. "Some of these people make millions!" She was convinced we could make some good money from this. Enough to get out of debt, pay for college, and—who knew?—maybe even get a little rich.

But Hayden Booth. Not even Mom, deep in the throes of *dream it, be it*, imagined Hayden Booth would come knocking.

When his office called to request a meeting, Mom was shaken. Almost scared. Like she'd been summoned by God.

When you read articles about Hayden Booth—which Mom did, obsessively, after he called—he was sometimes described as a music producer, other times a talent manager, other times a social media aggregator. "There wasn't a word for what I did before I came along," he bragged in one of those articles. "I just call myself a creator."

His origin story had become a thing of myth. Ten years ago he'd been a scrappy club kid from London, broke and backpacking through Berlin, when he saw this girl busking on the U-Bahn. He'd listened to her sing and play guitar and seen her entire trajectory right away. It was like a vision. He didn't know how, but he knew she could be huge, and he could be the one to get her there. When she finished singing, he approached her, not even knowing if she spoke English, and said, "I'm going to make you famous."

And he did.

He told us a version of that story at our first meeting, when, after having us wait for two hours in the reception area, he finally invited us into his office and sat us down on a bench that felt like concrete while he sat in his throne, backlit by the bank of windows behind him.

When he finished telling us how he'd made Lulia, and then Mélange, then Rufus Q, he said he was always on the hunt for who was next. He looked at me, eyes open and unblinking. It was terrifying. I cast my gaze around his office, in search of a safe haven, looking out the window, at the wall, at his weird graffiti art print that read: *Art is personal. Business is not*—anywhere but at Hayden.

Finally he asked: "Do you know what it means to be famous?"

Mom started to answer, but Hayden held up his hand and she went quiet. "From them."

There was a pause. Sabrina looked at me, her face uncharacteristically uncertain. "To be known for what you do?" Sabrina said at the same time I said, "To be loved."

"My CPA is known for having creative ways of hiding money from the IRS. Is he famous?" he asked Sabrina.

Sabrina shook her head.

"And my granny was beloved. But I bet you've never heard of Pauline Howarth, have you?" he asked my mother.

She shook her head.

"Most people don't know what fame is. They confuse fame with celebrity, celebrity with buzz. But I'm going to tell you how it works." He said this like he was divulging a secret.

He stood up and stalked around the desk, leaning on the edge of it closest to Sabrina. "First, you've got buzz." He cupped his left hand into the shape of a *C*. "You girls already have that. But buzz is cheap. It's your fifteen minutes of fame. It's what a daft woman in a Chewbacca suit gets. It comes and it goes. Unless . . ." Here he cupped his other hand into a *C*. "Buzz sustains enough to become celebrity. Which lasts a bit longer, but it's still built on quicksand. Now, if celebrity can be translated into commodity, you're onto something. You can dine out on that. Sports stars. B-list actors. Reality TV stars. Second-rate musicians get this far, an endless loop of buzz, celebrity, commodity."

Here he joined his two hands together so they made a circle, the fingers not quite touching. "You can ride that train pretty far, make a living that way, but it's still not fame." He paused. His fingers began to flutter, like wings of a bird wanting to take flight. "Mum here has done a bang-up job getting you girls this far. You two might even make some good money for a while, get some decent endorsements and revenue, but I promise you this: it won't last more than a few months or, if you're really lucky, years. But sooner or later—probably sooner—people will be on to the next shiny thing, and it won't be you. When that happens, your fans will forget you. Your numbers will drop. And you'll go back to being like everyone else."

"So how do we keep that from happening?" Mom asked.

"That brings us to fame," Hayden said, ignoring her. "Sometimes, if you're talented, if you have that something extra, and if you're surrounded by the right people, you stand a shot at breaking out of that loop. Out of celebrity, which is ephemeral . . ." Here he exploded his hands wide open, his bird fingers soaring to the heavens. "And into fame, which is eternal."

Hayden's phone began to ring, rattling on the desk. The screen flashed *Lulia*, as if the universe wanted to confirm what Hayden had said.

"Fame," Hayden continued. "That's what I do. I create fame. But only under the right circumstances, with the right artists. Those who are talented enough. And hungry enough." Here he stopped to look at me. "The question is: Are you hungry enough?"

I had no idea if I was hungry enough, what that even meant, what he was promising. But I had understood one thing. *Your numbers will drop. Your fans will forget you.* I knew what that meant.

"Are you hungry enough?" Hayden repeated.

Mom and Sabrina spoke as one, answering, as they always did, for me. "We are," they said.

THE ORDER OF LOSS
PART VI

HARUN

I found James because of a dollar bill and lost him because of a fifty. Which is oversimplifying, but how else do you explain something as inexplicable as love?

"Yo. You drop this?" I looked up. There was James, holding up a crumpled dollar bill.

"I don't think so," I stammered. It was my first week at the community college, and though the campus was small and in the city where I'd spent all my life, I was lost. Clutching my schedule and map, I was trying to find the building my statistics class would be held in.

I looked up from my printed schedule and saw his face for the first time. Everything about him seemed to suggest warmth: the glow of his dark skin, the goatee that made him look like he wore a permanent smile, the brown eyes, twinkling, like he was in on the best joke.

"Where you need to be?" he asked me.

And I had the strangest thought: *Right here is where I need to be.*

James grabbed the schedule. "You're at Newkirk. You need building G, on the other side of Bergen. Lemme show you," he said, and took me by my elbow, which subsequently caught fire.

I paid no attention in statistics that day. I just rubbed my still-tingling elbow and thought of the boy with the laughing eyes whose name I did not even catch and whom I would likely never see again. So when I came out of the building and saw him leaning against the bike racks, my first thought was that it was a miracle. Then I remembered it couldn't possibly be that. But when he asked me if I wanted to grab a coffee, it did seem like some sort of divine intervention.

We talked for two hours straight, pausing only to breathe. James told me he was in his second year of school, studying food management in hopes of becoming a chef. He watched cooking shows obsessively, and could take any five ingredients and turn them into something delicious. He was an only child, raised by his mom, until one weekend she dropped him off with his father and never came back. He'd recently moved out of his father's house, and was now crashing with a cousin in the Heights while he figured things out.

I told James that I was studying business and accounting in hopes of one day taking over—or, if Ammi had anything to say about it, expanding—my parents' auto supply business. I told him how Abu had gotten a green card from the lottery when he was nineteen, arriving at JFK with one suitcase. For ten years, he worked three jobs, sometimes twenty-hour days, sending money home each month and saving what he could until he had enough to buy a business. Only then did he go back home to find a wife.

I told him about Ammi, moving to a strange land to live with a husband she barely knew, arriving in winter, and feeling assaulted by the cold. She had cried every day and hadn't left the house until she saw the first crocus, at which point she'd walked to Abu's store and asked him to give her something to do. He'd taught her to do his accounting, and now she did it for so many businesses she had to turn down work. Abu sometimes joked that it was a good thing they were married, otherwise she'd have no time for his books.

At six, Ammi texted, wanting to know where I was. James and I exchanged phone numbers, and the rest of the week, we kept up the conversation via texts.

"Who're you texting?" Halima asked.

The lie flew out automatically. "Jabir."

"Is that a new friend from school?" Ammi asked.

"Yes," I said. That night, I changed James's name in my contacts to Jabir and started deleting his texts at the end of each day.

We met for coffee again, at my suggestion, away from campus, in one of those expensive cafés on the walking mall.

"You seeing anyone?" James asked me casually.

"Not at the moment," I said.

"Not at the moment?" he repeated, a teasing drawl, as if he already knew the truth.

"I've never . . . seen anyone," I admitted. "I've never done anything . . . with anyone."

For a second, I was scared he'd laugh at me, or reject me, but he just ran his finger across the rim of his coffee mug, nodding, as if it all made sense to him, as if *I* made sense to him.

"I take it you're not out to your family?" he asked.

"I'm not out to anyone."

"'Cept me."

The revelation stunned me, but in a good way, like I'd been a can of soda on a shelf, all quiet and dusty until someone had come along and shaken me. For the first time in my life, someone else knew who I was. The realization left me giddy, light-headed, drunk (or what I imagined drunk to be like).

"Except you," I told James.

James smiled and licked his lips. "Seeing as you told me a secret, I guess I owe you one back."

"You already told me about that singer you're obsessed with."

"Freya." He shook his head. "Nah. Not her." He cast his eyes downward, a little creep of red at his sideburns. He was embarrassed. I was a goner. "You didn't drop that dollar bill." He paused. "I did."

"You did? Why?"

His eyes were slow and sleepy, coming up to greet mine like a morning sunrise. "To meet you."

And with that, the can was shaken even harder, and the fizzy sensation grew more powerful than it had been that night with Aladdin, more powerful than it had been with all

the crushes on boys real and make-believe whom I'd fanta-
sized about over the years but never really allowed myself to
imagine being with.

"Got another secret for you," James said. He leaned across
the table and beckoned me closer. His mouth was near my
ear, his finger was on the tab. If he opened that can, there
would be no going back.

"What?" I asked. Entire body liquid.

"I'm gonna kiss you now," he whispered.

— — —

"I thought March was supposed to be in like a lion, out like a
lamb," James muttered that frigid day a year and a half later.
"And it's almost April. Ain't supposed to be this cold."

James wasn't living in Jersey anymore, not going to school
anymore, which was why we'd taken to meeting Thursdays
in the city. He complained that one day a week wasn't enough,
and I didn't like it either, but some days we were together ten
hours and I justified that, amortized over a week, it wasn't
that bad.

James hated the cold in general, but particularly on our
Thursdays, when it was a stinging reminder that we had no
place to go. He'd been kicked out of his father's place before I
met him and had been bouncing from friend to relative ever
since, first in the Heights, later on the Grand Concourse, and
now in Inwood with a sympathetic aunt who mostly worked
nights. "Come spend a night," he wheedled. I wanted to. But
I couldn't.

"You could if you told your family," James said.

"And how did that work out for you?"

It was a low blow—I'd since learned that the reason James didn't live with his father anymore was that his father kicked him out after James told him he was gay—but it illustrated my point. And for this reason, it usually shut James up.

When it was cold outside, we'd meet and go to a café, station ourselves there for hours, and dream about being somewhere else. "One day, we'll go to Brazil. Or to Fiji," James would say. He'd seen pictures of tree houses in the Amazon, Fijian bungalows perched right over water as blue as a swimming pool. He'd pull up the images on his phone and show me. "You'll be a pilot and fly us everywhere we want to go," he said, even though James knew I'd long since put away my dreams of being a pilot, long since stopped plane-watching.

Sometimes I tried to picture us hiking through the rain forests, diving into that impossibly blue water, but it was like trying to read a book in a dream: I could never quite see it.

That cold spring day, Fiji seemed farther away than ever. I steered James toward the nearest Starbucks, knowing a hot chocolate and a warm corner were the best we could do.

But he didn't want to go there. He didn't want to go anywhere. "I'm tired of this," he muttered.

Tired of this was a fist to the gut. *Tired of this* really meant tired of me.

"Is it because I'm black?" James asked. "Christian? Can't do nothing about black, but I could convert. I had an uncle who was Nation of Islam for a while."

It took me a moment to understand what he was saying. That he thought his not being a Muslim was the deal breaker with my family.

"That wouldn't help."

"At least I'm willing to try," he said.

"You think they'd invite you for dinner? Be happy for us to have sleepovers?" I shook my head, angry. "My mother didn't speak to my brother for six months after he married a white *woman*."

"So you just gonna keep doing like this? Keep lying to them, and to yourself, because you're too chickenshit to be true?"

"How am I lying to myself?"

"Everything you do is to keep playing the good, dutiful son, and it's all bullshit." He stopped and looked at me with a withering disgust. "Did you ever even tell your parents you wanted to be a pilot?"

"What does that have to do with anything? All little kids have things they want to be when they grow up. Abdullah wanted to be Bob the Builder! Halima wanted to be a Disney princess. It doesn't mean that's what you're going to do. And anyway, it's not like any American carrier would be eager to hire a pilot named Harun Siddiqui."

"See!" James said, jabbing me with his delicate finger. "That's just it. You write people off without giving them a chance."

"No," I said. "I live in reality."

James grunted and walked ahead of me. He abruptly

stopped, which I thought meant he was ready to make up. He never could stay angry long. But he stooped down and picked something up. It was a fifty-dollar bill.

My first thought was that he'd done it on purpose, but I knew James did not have spare fifties lying around. And I could tell by the surprised smile on his face that he hadn't dropped it. He'd found it.

"We should see if someone lost it," I said.

"And let someone else take it?" He shook his head. "Aww, hell no."

"It's stealing," I said.

"It ain't stealing. It's finding. Anyone might've dropped it, but *we* found it."

"It's still wrong."

"Think of it as a gift from God."

"You don't believe in God," I said.

"Nah, boo. You're the one who don't believe in God."

"Why would you say that?"

"Because you got no faith."

I didn't know *what* to do with that.

"Got any cash on you?" he asked.

I had twenty and some change. James started tapping away on his phone. "Between us we got almost ninety. There's gotta be some cheap-ass hotel that rents rooms for that much." He tapped some more on his phone, and then his face broke out into that wide-toothed smile. "Place near Penn Station, says it's only ninety-three a night."

"We don't have ninety-three."

"Close though. Come on."

We walked to the hotel, the wind, gritty and mean, pushing back against us.

The hotel clerk told us the room was actually $125 a night, plus tax, but if we paid cash and left by the end of his shift and didn't use the towels, we could have it for eighty.

We rode the elevator to the ninth floor. James was shaking when we unlocked the door, but he said it was on account of the cold, and the first thing he did was crank up the thermostat.

The room was ugly and dark, with a window that looked out onto an air shaft. When I imagined us being someplace together, it didn't look like this. Or like the tropical waters in Fiji. It looked like my house, my bed.

That was *my* running-away fantasy. To be able to sleep like spoons in my bed at home, with James, not hiding. But that seemed so much further away than the Fijian bungalow.

We sat on opposite ends of the bed. We'd wanted this for so long, a place to be together, and now we had it and didn't know what to do.

It wasn't like we hadn't had sex. In the hidden corners of Central Park, in the empty ladies' lounge on the top floor of one of the city's old, failing department stores, we had explored the hidden reaches of each other's bodies. But those encounters were, by necessity, always fast and furtive: shirts yanked up, zippers yanked down, the important bits exposed but always both of us ready to make a break for it.

In truth, I was that way with James: always ready to make a break for it.

But here, in this room, with the thermostat cranked, we could take our time. Tentatively, we started to kiss, giggling nervously. We kicked off our shoes. We kissed some more, a little steadier, and peeled off our shirts. We went slow, even though it was agonizing, because for once, we could.

By taking our time, I saw things I'd never seen. A rigid scar on his left shoulder. The way the skin of his belly was a different color from the rest of him, more like my tone than his. His feet, the toes all the same length.

"My mom used to call them my ballerina feet," he said when I commented on them.

"You never talk about your mom."

"Nothing to say."

"Did you love her?"

"What kind of question is that? Course I loved her." He paused to bite his thumbnail. "And I know she loved me, but sometimes that ain't enough."

"You always tell me that love is all you need," I said.

"Maybe I should start living in reality too," he replied.

I got that bad feeling again.

"I love you," I told him. "You know that, right?"

"But not enough to do something about it. Not enough to risk anything. I told my pops. I didn't think about the consequences."

"That's not fair," I replied. "You told your father before

we met. And, I might remind you, he kicked you out."

"'I might remind you,'" he mimicked. "Like I could forget. And I told my pops knowing that one day I'd meet someone like you and when it happened I'd be ready."

The heater ticked off. The room went cold. I knew what he meant, or what he thought he meant. He told his father to make a place for me. But all I heard in that *someone like you* was someone other than me.

"Nothin's gonna change if you're not willing to change it," he said. "And if you aren't, we're gonna keep hiding out, paying off clerks for five hours in a hotel."

"Four hours now," I said. "And this was your idea."

"Fine. You wanna fuck?" He unzipped his pants, tugged on mine.

At that moment, I wanted the chill in the room to go away. I wanted the distance between us to shrink. I wanted to buy a few more minutes of borrowed time. So I told him yes, I did want to fuck.

He lunged for me, and I lunged for him. I didn't know if we were fighting or apologizing, declaring ourselves or saying goodbye, fucking or making love.

Maybe all of those.

After, we fell asleep curled into each other, like spoons.

I woke up, my phone lighting up with calls. It was Ammi. It was after six. I was meant to be home.

I left James in that hotel room, ran to the PATH, and ran home. I tried to imagine what it would be like to tell my parents. But it was like the Fijian bungalow; it existed somewhere out there in the world, but nowhere I could ever get to.

I got home late, concocting some lie to Ammi about losing track of time while studying for a big exam, and braced myself, as I did every Thursday, for the moment when Ammi would see through my lie with that radar of hers that allowed her to find a missing five dollars in her clients' books, to sniff out any remotely fishy business in their ledgers. But it never happened. She believed me because, unlike the people whose books she did, she trusted me.

I pushed the food around my plate, making another excuse about how we'd had pizza during the study session. She frowned but took my plate, and I ran to the shower to rinse James off my skin.

In my bedroom, I checked my phone, but there was no text from James. I was logging on to the computer to see if he'd sent me a Facebook message when Abu popped his head in. I quickly minimized the screen.

"Everything okay?" he asked.

For the millionth time, I tried to imagine what it would be like to tell him. *I am in love*, I could say. *His name is James.*

"Can I ask you something?"

"You can ask me anything."

"Why did Ammi get so angry when Saif married Leesa?"

"That woman does not always make it so easy."

"I know, but Ammi was angry before she even met her."

Abu sighed and came to sit down on the edge of Abdullah's bed. "You must understand, *beta*," he told me. "Your mother left her family behind to move to America. And sometimes

she feels like America is making strangers of her children."
He paused and smiled. "Why? Have you met a girl?"

I am in love. His name is James.

"No," I said, for once telling the truth.

Facebook pinged with a message, and my heart surged
with the thought of talking to James. "I should get back to
my work."

The message was not from James but from my cousin
Amir. We had not seen each other since that time he came
to America, but over the past few years we had reconnected
online.

How are you doing, cousin? read the message.

Not so good, I wrote.

He was online, even though it was five in the morning
there. I saw the dots as he typed. Tell me what is wrong.
Inshallah, I can help.

The words I could not confess to my father rose up in me,
desperate for an audience, and my cousin, ten thousand miles
away, the seed of it all, seemed not only safe but like *qismat*,
like fate.

3

HUNGER

As they're finishing up at the urgent care clinic, awaiting Nathaniel's discharge papers, the doctor asks Freya for her number. And even though the doctor has provided ample evidence that he is both incompetent and a creep, and even though Freya's creep radar is so finely tuned she could sell it to the CIA, the request does something to her heart. She designated herself Nathaniel's emergency contact, and now the doctor is officially assigning her that role.

Freya is never in charge of anyone. Someone has always been in charge of her: first her father, then Sabrina, now Hayden. She writes down her number for the doctor, a little embarrassed by this surge of good feeling.

She is Nathaniel's emergency contact. For today, anyhow, she is in charge of him. She no longer cares about whether or not he will sue her or whether Harun will sell her pictures. She is someone's person.

After Freya hands him the paper, the doctor folds it into a square and deposits it into the breast pocket of his lab coat and with a smarmy smile asks: "You like martinis?" It takes Freya a moment to realize that she got it wrong (what else is new?) and the doctor is hitting on her.

Freya is an empty vessel once again, emptier yet for having been, at least momentarily, full. Just like that, she's in a foul temper—extreme moodiness is evidence of diva mode, per her mother—feeling worse than she did after the miracle doctor sent her away with no miracle. Worse than she did in the park after she'd seen Alex Takashida's Facebook post (*She said yes!*).

Freya never gets asked questions she wants to say yes to. Freya is in charge of no one. Freya is liked by millions, needed by none.

Fuck it. She no longer cares if Harun has pictures of her on his phone. Let him sell them. Why shouldn't he cash in on her somewhere-between-buzz-and-celebrity status before it's too late? Someone ought to.

Her mother was right. She should just go home and watch *Scandal*.

Except she doesn't want to go home and watch *Scandal*. She doesn't want to do anything. The last few weeks have been bleak. Whole desolate stretches of hours. The thing that used to soothe her—logging on, chatting with her fans, or at least seeing what they were saying about her—now torments her. She can't stop hearing Hayden's prophecy: *your fans will forget you, your numbers will drop, you'll go back to being like everyone else.*

"So," she says to Nathaniel. "Where are you headed?"

"Guess I'll meet my dad," Nathaniel replies unsteadily.

This is the most she's heard him speak, so at least he isn't brain damaged. Though he still seems pretty dazed, and looking at him makes her feel, bewilderingly, homesick.

"Are you staying with friends? At a hotel? Or Airbnb?"

No response.

"Or does your father live here?"

"Uhh. My dad's taken care of that."

Is it her, or is he not making a lot of sense? She looks at Harun, cocks her head to the side. He gives the slightest of nods.

"Maybe you should call your father," Harun suggests.

"I don't want to worry him," Nathaniel says.

"I don't think you should be out wandering alone after a concussion," Harun says.

"Right!" Freya says, remembering something from a TV show. Was it *Grey's Anatomy*? She and Sabrina used to watch that together religiously. "In case you fall asleep."

"Fall asleep?"

"It's dangerous to fall asleep," Freya says. She has no idea if this is accurate, but as Hayden would say, the truth is how you sell it. "You might not wake up."

"The doctor didn't say anything about that," Nathaniel says in slow, measured words. "He wasn't even sure it was a concussion."

"The doctor was incompetent," Harun says. "When my brother Abdullah was concussed, he was told not to go to sleep without supervision, in case he had a subdural hematoma. If you get those, you die." Harun turns to Nathaniel. "You wouldn't want that to happen, would you?"

When Nathaniel doesn't answer, Freya answers for him: "No," she says. "You wouldn't."

— — —

Now that Nathaniel's head is clearing, he's more confused than ever.

He understands what happened to him. The girl, Freya, fell onto him, and the other guy—Harun?—saw it go down, but what he doesn't understand is what they're still doing here.

He gets why they didn't leave him in the park, though he wouldn't have been surprised or even all that disappointed if they had. And he understands why they took him to a doctor and even paid for the doctor—they felt guilty and obligated.

But whatever debt there was has been paid. They're free to go. He's told them it's all good so many times.

And yet they're still here.

Which unnerves him. Almost as much as the questions they continue to fire at him. Because after warning him about his imminent death—which made him almost laugh—they started quizzing him about his plans, asking for specifics— wheres, whens, addresses, things for which Nathaniel has not prepared.

"Maybe we should wait until you talk to your father," Freya says.

Nathaniel is not by nature a deceptive person, but he's

learned a few tricks over the years to throw people off the trail, to protect his father, to protect himself.

Nathaniel pulls out his phone. "Oh, look. He left me a message."

"I didn't hear the phone ring," says Harun.

"The ringer's off."

They don't make it easy, these two. Nathaniel excuses himself and puts on a big show of listening to the voicemail and calling his father back and talking to dead air. *Yeah*, he says to his father, saying how great it is to be in New York City. *Me too*, he replies when his dad says he's looking forward to seeing him. After a minute or two of this he hangs up and returns to the others.

"So?" Harun says.

"He says we can meet earlier," Nathaniel says.

"Now?" Harun asks.

Nathaniel nods.

"Maybe we should escort him up there," Harun says to Freya. "Hand him off."

It's getting worse and worse. Why are they so persistent?

"Well, not *now* now," Nathaniel says, tripping over his story. "In a few hours. He's busy."

"Busy? Did you not tell him you were concussed?" Harun demands. He seems affronted by Nathaniel's father's perceived neglect. And Nathaniel feels that age-old instinct to protect his father flare up.

"I didn't tell him," he says. "I didn't want to worry him."

He expects an argument from Harun, who has been a fierce interrogator so far, but he just nods at this, as if in agreement about the need to not worry fathers unnecessarily.

"Let me at least get you a car," Freya says.

They've wasted enough time and money on him already. But if he accepts the car, they'll be done with him.

"Okay," he agrees.

"Where are you headed?"

"Umm, 175th Street," Nathaniel guesses.

"Where are you staying?" Freya asks.

"With friends of my dad's."

They seem to accept this, but Nathaniel is still uneasy. What if they want to come with him? What if they want to meet his dad?

"What's the address?" she asks.

Why are they doing this? He's given them every opportunity to leave. Why are they making it so hard? He knows that they are nice people who mean well, but don't they know that once you start feeding a stray cat, it will come back, it will depend on you?

He doesn't have an address. Can he make one up? Like 43 175th Street? Is that a place?

"My Uber's not working," Freya says, slapping her phone against her thigh.

Reprieve. Nathaniel exhales. "I can just take the subway."

"No," she says in a harsh voice. "I'll put you in a cab and give the driver cash."

She steps out into the street to hail a cab, and Nathaniel

watches her. She raises her hand confidently, as if certain she will be seen. Nathaniel wonders what that must feel like.

Though he's engineered his departure, he's already mourning the absence of this formidable girl, this persistent boy. He's seeing them disappear through the rear window of a taxi. He's feeling the leaden weight of his solitude. At least he'll see his father soon.

Freya jumps back onto the curb, holding her foot in her hand, cursing. Droplets of blood fall on the sidewalk. A shard of green glass glints from her heel.

"Are you okay?" Harun asks.

"I guess there's a reason people don't go barefoot in the city," she says ruefully, hopping on one foot.

"That looks pretty bad," Harun says. "Maybe you should go back to the urgent care?"

"No way. That doctor was a grade A douche, and they'll charge a hundred dollars for a piece of gauze." She glances at her foot. The blood is staining her jeans. "Fabulous. I look like a homeless serial killer."

Normally, Nathaniel carries a first aid kit with him at all times; he started carrying one after the thing with his eye. Probably a strip of gauze and some Neosporin wouldn't have changed anything, but it's better to be prepared. But he left his kit at home. He didn't see the point of being prepared.

"I can fix it for you," Nathaniel says. "We just need some gauze and wipes."

"There's a pharmacy across the street," Harun says.

The three of them cross the street, a wobbly chain like

before but with the order shuffled: where once a shaky Nathaniel was flanked by Freya and Harun, now Freya is hopping between them. She keeps insisting she's fine, but that's a lie Nathaniel can see through.

Harun offers to get supplies, and so Nathaniel stays outside with Freya and her bloody foot.

"I'm so sorry," he tells her.

"Why are *you* sorry?" she asks in a sharp voice.

"Because it's my fault."

"How is this your fault?"

"I threw up on your shoes."

"You threw up because I fell on you," she replies. "If anyone should be apologizing, it's me."

"No," Nathaniel says.

"No?"

"Don't apologize. I'm glad you fell on me."

"Why would you be glad I fell on you?" she asks.

Because you can't fall on something that doesn't exist, he thinks. He may be feral, but he's not been out of the world so long that he doesn't know this is a profoundly odd thing to say. So he doesn't say it.

— — —

Inside the pharmacy, Harun buys more supplies than necessary. To his mind, if he assembles the right first aid kit, he can keep Freya around for a little while longer, enough time to figure out how to get her in front of James, who's clearly blocked him and won't see any texts, and even if he did, probably wouldn't believe him. Once James sees Freya in the flesh, though, he'll have to understand that it's a sign that they should be together.

He puts a bottle of hydrogen peroxide in his basket, a box of bandages, a roll of gauze, some medical tape, Neosporin, and a pair of scissors. He passes over the generic products for the more expensive name brands because it's Freya. All together, it comes to almost thirty dollars, and he pays from the stash of money he purloined from his trip fund. It feels good to do something slightly worthy with the money, even if his intentions aren't so noble. But he'd like to think that he would be helping out in the same way even if it weren't Freya. Only maybe he would've bought the cheaper bandages.

— — —

As Freya sits on a cement planter, Nathaniel uses the scissors to extract the glass still lodged in her foot. He gently cleans the area with the hydrogen peroxide, and though he knows this must sting, Freya does not even flinch.

Formidable, he thinks.

He slathers her foot in ointment and slowly wraps the heel in gauze.

He takes his time. Because he is methodical by nature, but also because it feels incredibly good to touch another human being, and particularly this human being. It has been such a long time, and as he holds Freya's foot against his knee, getting some of her blood on the front of his jeans, where it will match the drop of her blood on his shirt from when he wiped her face before, he feels something hatching inside him. He pictures a bird, all tiny and helpless. He remembers when a nest fell out of the eaves of their house and he and his father tried to save the chicks, feeding them with eyedroppers. "Hope is the thing with feathers," his father had said, quoting Emily Dickinson, but then the birds had died and Nathaniel had realized that it was actually grief that was the thing with feathers.

He doesn't want to hope. He can't afford to hope. But there it is, the fluttering in his chest, all because a pretty girl (a beautiful girl) with beautiful eyes (sad eyes) is letting him hold her bare foot as he dresses a wound that he himself caused.

He doesn't want to hope. But he doesn't want to let go just yet. Is there some middle ground, a space where he can allow himself this bit of human kindness without getting too attached? It's so easy to get attached. Three baby birds, a shoebox, and an eyedropper. They'd buried the birds not far from where Mary's ashes were scattered. His father had wept.

Freya's foot is bandaged and taped, but Nathaniel can't quite let her go. Just a few minutes more. His father won't mind. He has lost the battle, and hope has won, and the desperation to get away has reversed itself. Because of a foot. A foot he can't seem to let go of. A foot that, miraculously, is still resting in his lap.

He stares at the foot of this formidable girl and holds his breath, because if he moves so much as an inch he will break the spell and Freya will surely leave.

— — —

The spell goes both ways. Freya can't move either. Doesn't want to move. Nathaniel may be holding on to her filthy foot, but it feels like he's palming her heart. It feels like she has a heart.

Please don't let go, she thinks.

— — —

Nathaniel doesn't let go.

— — —

Harun doesn't want to let go, either. "Maybe we should get you some shoes," he suggests. Freya *does* need shoes. But more to the point, her buying shoes will buy him time. "There's a store down the block."

— — —

"Shoes!" Nathaniel says. What a brilliant idea. He could hug Harun. "I need to buy you shoes."

"Oh, that's okay," Freya says, pulling her foot back.

"No," Nathaniel says, yanking her foot toward him. "I have to replace the ones I ruined."

"I didn't even like those shoes," she says. "You did me a favor."

He doesn't care if she liked them or not. He's the one who needs the favor. He needs this. Just for a little longer. Is it too much to ask? Probably. But he's asking anyway.

"I *have* to buy you shoes."

Freya's foot stiffens, and Nathaniel knows he's revealed a part of himself that must be kept secret. The wild, feral part that Dad said they could show each other but not anyone else (*Don't tell your mother*) because they wouldn't understand. Nathaniel tries to remember the person he once was, athletic, even popular. He tries faking being him. "It's just the right thing to do, to get you new shoes, you know?" His voice sounds strange and foreign, like someone on TV. Is she buying it? Can he pass as his old self? Was he ever his old self?

"I really don't need you to buy me shoes," Freya says.

She starts to pull her leg away, but Nathaniel can't let go. He's a drowning man, and her ankle is his life preserver. But she's pulling it away, leaving him no choice but to reveal the feral man inside. "Please," he begs. "Let me buy you shoes."

— — —

Freya doesn't need new shoes. At home, she has rows of them; many of them, like the pair she threw away earlier, had been given to her in hopes of a mention online. It used to thrill her, all the freebies in exchange for her word. But now that she knows it all might go away soon, it's like wearing shoes made of lead.

In any event, she doesn't need Nathaniel to buy her shoes. Certainly not $375 shoes, which was what the ones he puked on today cost. She wonders if he even has $375 to his name.

She pictures his wallet, the lonely bills, the creased photo strip, the folded business card. She glances at his shoes, a pair of dirty canvas sneakers that she would bet $375 have holes in the soles.

— — —

This is a bet she would win.

— — —

And that's when she understands: he is her responsibility. He is, for today anyway, her person. She doesn't need new shoes, but she needs this to continue. So if Nathaniel wants to buy her shoes, she'll let him buy her shoes.

"Okay," she says. "Let's get me shoes."

— — —

Who is made happier by this statement? Harun, Nathaniel, or Freya? Hard to tell.

— — —

The store Harun pointed to is a chain, the kind of place Freya used to shop in but hasn't in years because *dream it, be it.*

It's empty, and there are comfy seats inside, but Freya gestures to the bench outside. "You wait out here." It comes out as a command. She's told that she can come across as imperious, bitchy. She's read people sniping about this. *She needed us when she started out, but now she's too good*, they write. *No,* Freya wants to reply. *I still need you.* But she wasn't permitted to respond anymore, and so the silence seemed to confirm their suspicions. Anyway, Hayden told her not to worry about it. Some early fans would always feel betrayed when their secret got out. This did not make Freya feel better. She didn't want to betray anyone else.

But she doesn't want Nathaniel coming into the shoe store, because she has no intention of spending the fifty-dollar bill he's thrust into her hand. So she softens her voice and says: "Girls and shoes can take a while."

It's the first time Freya sees Nathaniel smile.

"Take all the time you need," he says, and he looks like he means it, which must be a first among the ranks of young men.

"Yes, no rush at all," Harun adds.

A second.

She leaves them there and goes inside, surveying the inventory, inhaling the smell of new leather.

"See anything you like?" the clerk asks.

Before Freya goes out for an event, she and her mother consult a series of photographs a stylist has shot for them, different outfit combinations for different occasions. Never the same thing twice. Sometimes she likes the clothes, sometimes she doesn't, but she always feels as though she's playing dress-up. "That's the point," says her mother, who sounds more like Hayden every day.

Freya scans the shoes and stops at a pair of orange flats with thick rubber soles. She flips them over. Eighty dollars but half off. When Nathaniel pressed the fifty into her hand, she took it, but only to placate him, figuring she'd find a way to give it back later. Still, it feels right to stay within Nathaniel's budget. "I'll take these in a size eight," she calls to the clerk.

While she waits for the shoes, she pulls out her phone, but before she looks at it, her gaze is drawn to the window. Outside, Harun and Nathaniel sit side by side, hands folded into their laps, like obedient children waiting for their mother. Looking at the pair of them, she feels another lurch in her chest.

She puts her phone away. The clerk brings the shoes, and Freya slips them on. They fit perfectly. Freya pays with her credit card and returns to the boys.

"I'm famished," Freya announces when she returns to the boys, even though she's not remotely hungry. "Where should we eat?"

She uses her imperious voice in the hope that it makes it sound like lunch has been on the books for weeks. She's trying to hide the fact that if these two strangers say no, Freya, who has millions of friends, won't have a single soul to keep her company today.

She looks at Harun. He's been her ally so far today. Will he come along?

"There's a diner nearby," he says, and Freya wants to hug him. "I've been there before. It's not too expensive, not that you . . ." He stumbles and reddens. "The food's good, and they don't care if you stay a while."

"Perfect," Freya says. Harun stands up. Nathaniel remains seated.

"Are you coming?" Freya asks. Part of being a good vocalist is making your voice project feelings you don't necessarily possess, so Freya makes her voice sound authoritative even though she is sick at the prospect that Nathaniel will say no and her whole flimsy plan will collapse and they'll go their separate ways, leaving Freya all alone.

"Unless you're not hungry?" Harun says when Nathaniel doesn't answer. Freya wants to smack him for even giving Nathaniel the opening of an out. Doesn't he see how hard she's trying? How much she needs this?

"No, I'm hungry," Nathaniel admits.

— — —

Nathaniel is not hungry. He is ravenous. He hasn't eaten a hot meal in more than two weeks. More than that, he hasn't shared a meal with another person in two weeks.

But that's not the kind of thing you say. Not out loud. Not when the going is, at least temporarily, good.

— — —

Nathaniel is hungry. Freya is ridiculously relieved. "Cool," she says, toning down her enthusiasm now that agreement has been reached. "Let's go eat."

— — —

The waiter at the diner is a crabby old Greek whose rudeness never wavers, whether you order a cup of tea or a steak dinner (which James did one time for them to share—a mistake, in retrospect—it had the consistency of rope), who administers a fish eye whether you eat and go within a half hour or stay for hours. For this reason, it was one of their favorite spots.

James would flirt with the waiter, even though it never made a dent. Still, he was determined. "I can win anyone over," he said, giving Harun a look to show just which anyone he was referring to.

There's no reason to think he might be here. Even though it's a Thursday. James probably didn't come downtown today. Why would he? But if he had, if he were here . . . Harun imagines it. Walking in with Freya. Delivering James this gift. He would not be able to refuse it. They would kiss. The crabby waiter would finally smile.

James isn't here. The waiter is frowning.

The place is mostly empty. One old guy who's always at the counter. A booth full of girls. The table in the corner— the one they sat at because it was next to the bathroom and seemed the least desirable and therefore the least objectionable to commandeer for whole afternoons of ordering only soup—is empty.

They sit down in a booth. The cranky waiter delivers the menus with a long-suffering sigh and slaps down three waters, sloshing them all over the Manhattan-map placemats.

The menu is a species typical of New York diners, which is to say pages and pages long with laminated pictures of food that are always much more appetizing than the real-life offerings. Harun normally gets the soup. There is only so wrong you can go with soup. Also, a bowl of soup costs five dollars and the cranky waiter is oddly generous with the crackers.

Nathaniel stares at the smudged pictures of omelets and burgers and skyscraper sandwiches with deep concentration. Freya, who claimed to be so hungry, hasn't even looked at the menu. She's frowning at her phone.

"Order?" the waiter asks, tapping his pen against the pad as if he has dozens of other places to be, dozens of other tables to service.

"I'll have the minestrone soup," Harun says.

"Cup or bowl?"

"Cup."

The waiter grunts. "You?" he asks Nathaniel.

Nathaniel is looking at the menu with a bewildered expression. "Uhh, the same, I guess."

Ammi sometimes talked about what it was like when she moved to America to marry Abu. She'd studied English in school, but it turned out to be completely insufficient for carrying on actual conversations. She learned by parroting what the natives said. When Harun realizes that's exactly what Nathaniel just did, he deeply regrets ordering the soup.

"I'll have a Cobb salad, no bacon, no egg, dressing on the side," Freya says, looking about as pleased with her order as Harun is with his.

"Two cups of minestrone and a dry Cobb," the waiter repeats, already starting to leave.

He's halfway back to the kitchen when Freya calls out, "Wait. I changed my mind."

Harun braces for the waiter's ire. And sure enough, he

returns with a murderous expression on his face.

"Sorry," Freya says, smiling at him, as if trying the "kill 'em with kindness" strategy. It doesn't work for her either.

"I'd like a grilled cheese on rye bread with tomatoes." She licks her lips. "And American cheese. It has to be American."

"Salad or fries?" the waiter asks.

Freya hesitates for a second. "Fuck it," she decides. "Fries. Extra crispy."

"Extra crispy?" the waiter asks.

"Yeah, put them through the deep fryer twice."

The waiter appears horrified by this.

"And a side of honey."

"Honey?"

"For the fries."

The waiter looks even more horrified.

Freya smiles.

Harun looks at Nathaniel, gaunt Nathaniel, and feels his hunger as if it were his own, though his appetite vanished when James told him to get the fuck out his life. Knowing the risks, he calls the waiter back. By the look on his face, Harun is fairly certain one of them is going to have their meal adorned with a healthy side of spit.

"I would like the same as her," Harun says.

"You want what she's having?" The waiter is incredulous, as if he knows that Harun doesn't even like grilled cheese sandwiches.

"Exactly. Fries extra crispy."

"You want honey too?"

"Sure," Harun says. He looks at Nathaniel, thinks of Ammi doing as the natives do. "Should we just make it three?"

There's a look on Nathaniel's face—relief, gratitude—and Harun wonders why it fills him with shame.

— — —

When the food comes, Nathaniel is overcome by the force of his appetite. His last meal was six bags of airplane pretzels stolen off the cart and hastily eaten in the tiny lavatory.

He's nearly undone by the tastes of the food. The ooze of melting cheese on his tongue, the tiny caraway seeds that explode under the force of his molars, the delightful sweetness of honey with french fries, which Freya has insisted both he and Harun try, holding the fry so close to Nathaniel's mouth that it is a minor miracle he doesn't eat her finger too.

It's only when he looks up and sees Freya and Harun staring at him with similarly peculiar expressions that he understands he has done something wrong, revealed the wild man within him (*Don't tell your mother*). He looks down at his barren plate. He's devoured everything: the sandwich, the fries, the pickle, even the wilted lettuce that he realizes was meant for garnish. Meanwhile, neither Freya nor Harun has eaten even half of their sandwiches.

He is mortified. He's been too long out of this world. He's become uncivilized.

Just us, buddy.

Wordlessly, Harun takes half of his sandwich and puts it on Nathaniel's plate. Freya does the same.

Nathaniel protests, but they cut him off.

"I'm not hungry," Harun says.

"Neither am I," Freya admits.

Nathaniel stares at his magically replenished plate. "If you weren't hungry, why did you order all this food?" he asks.

There's a pause as Freya and Harun glance at each other. Then they look at him. "Because you were," they say.

— — —

Nathaniel excuses himself to use the bathroom.

There, in a stall no bigger than the one on the airplane where he consumed his last meal, he pinches the skin above his nose to keep the tears from coming.

Then he pulls out his phone and calls his father.

— — —

When he comes out, something is different.

For one, a cluster of girls surrounds the table. But the thing that's really changed is Freya. He doesn't know how to explain it, only that she looks like a different person. He steps tentatively closer and hears the girls squealing, recalling how the girls at school used to cheer like that when he hit a fly ball deep into left field, back when he was at least half a human.

"Oh my god, it *is* you!" one of the girls is saying. "I *told* you so! I told you it was her," she tells her friends.

"I know. But, like, what is *Freya* doing in *our* diner?"

"Can we get your autograph?" the third girl asks, brandishing a pen.

"Sure," Freya says.

A piece of binder paper is produced. "Can you do one to Violet. One to McKenzie, capital *M*, capital *K*, and no *a*. And one to Gia. That's me."

"Her real name is Gina."

"Shut up!" Gia/Gina turns to Freya. "Gia is my stage name."

Freya nods.

"Is Freya a stage name?" Gia asks.

"Nope," she says.

"You're so lucky to have such a good name."

Freya smiles a tight smile, hands the paper back.

"I'm going to get this framed," Gia says.

"Put it somewhere safe," McKenzie says. "It's going to be worth money when she becomes huge."

To this, Freya frowns.

"Not that I'll sell your autograph," McKenzie quickly corrects.

When the autographs are done, the girls ask for a selfie. Freya has to get out of the booth to arrange herself with them. Nathaniel takes the opportunity to sit down next to Harun.

"What's happening?" he asks.

"They're fans."

"Fans of what?"

"Freya."

Nathaniel is also a fan of Freya. He's become quite a big fan in the past few hours, but he still doesn't understand who these girls are.

"Have you not heard of Freya?" Harun asks.

Nathaniel shakes his head.

Harun shows Nathaniel a video on his phone. There, on the tiny screen, but somehow larger than life, is Freya.

"It's an older song," Harun says. "It's James's . . ." he stops. "It's my favorite."

Nathaniel glances at Harun's phone, back at Freya, back at the girl on the screen.

"That's her?" he asks Harun.

"I know. Of all the people to fall on you."

But that's not what he means. He doesn't know how to reconcile this person on the screen with the person in the park who whispered his name, who knew things about him.

According to Harun, though, Freya is apparently some sort of singer, known, beloved. He only half hears this because he's fixated on the person on the screen. How is she the same person he's been with all afternoon? And why does this song sound familiar? Where would he have heard it?

As if the on-screen Freya has registered his disbelief, she stops playing piano and turns toward the camera. As she taps out a beat on the piano bench, singing without accompaniment, she once again becomes the Freya Nathaniel recognizes. In a warm, husky voice that sounds like the one that whispered into Nathaniel's ear before, she sings:

If you can't see
Turn to me.
I see well enough
For the both of us.

Everything around him goes quiet, and for a second, Nathaniel is back in the forest, blindfolded, and when he returns
to the diner, he is certain that this song was written for him.
Obviously, it wasn't. He's never met Freya before, and why
would she, or anyone, write a song for him? But for that one
fleeting second, he's as sure of this as he is of anything in his
life.

The girls, having procured their autographs and photographs, begin to depart, but after a brief whispered conference they are back.

"Okay, you can totally say no," Gia says, "but we usually
come here with our friend Sasha. Like, every day. It's our
spot. So normally Sasha would be with us today. But she's
sick, so she didn't come to school."

"And it's her birthday," Violet adds.

"That's too bad," Freya says, "to be sick on your birthday."

"I know, right? She's going to die when she hears what she
missed."

Freya nods, commiserating.

"Could you, like, record her a message?"

"Please!" McKenzie says.

"Sure."

Gia aims the phone at Freya. "Hi, Sasha. Hope you feel better and have a happy birthday."

The girls exchange a look. "Could you maybe sing for her?" Gia asks.

Nathaniel feels it, a lurch in his gut, before he looks up and sees that Freya, who has been good-natured and generous, suddenly looks pained.

"I don't think so," she is saying.

"Nothing major. Just sing 'Happy Birthday.'"

Freya hesitates, the look on her face traveling from discomfort to despair, a route Nathaniel knows so well he could traverse it blindfolded.

"And we wouldn't post it on social media or anything," Violet promises.

"Umm, I really don't think I should," Freya says.

Nathaniel hears the song again. It's already familiar, something he's always known.

— — —

"Well, that was very rude," Harun says after the girls leave. "You were so nice to them, and they just kept asking for more."

He sounds like James, who would sometimes monitor how people were reacting to Freya as if he were her personal protector. Which, to his mind, he was. He'd discovered Freya singing "I Will Survive" the day his father kicked him out of the house, and he felt like she was singing to him. He'd posted something in the comments, not something he'd ever done before or since: *Not sure I WILL survive.* And Freya herself had replied: *Yes, you will. You might not believe it, but I do.* And from that moment on, James was all in.

"And asking you to sing. Do you even think there is a Sasha?" Harun continues. "I mean, you're not some performing monkey, are you?" he adds, even though forty minutes ago, he had imagined James being in the diner and Freya singing one of her songs for him and James forgiving him. "That must get so tiresome. Sometimes you must wish for everyone to leave you alone."

— — —

This is not what she wishes. It's what she fears.

Your numbers will drop. Your fans will forget you.

And then what? Who's left?

Freya looks down and begins to cry.

— — —

Nathaniel reaches out and brushes the tear from Freya's cheek.

I see well enough
For the both of us.

And at that moment, Nathaniel hears well enough for the both of them.

"You can't sing," Nathaniel says.

— — —

Freya has been ordered not to tell anyone about her current issues. Hayden has warned her that it alters the narrative they've worked so hard to create for Freya. Freya is tough. Freya is unstoppable. Freya is destiny. "Don't tell anyone. Not your fans or your friends," Hayden warned.

What friends? Her fans are her friends.

She looks at Nathaniel and Harun, staring at her with a mix of terror and tenderness. Staring at her not like strangers but something like friends.

"I can't sing," she says.

— — —

"What do you mean you can't sing?" Harun is distraught. If Freya can't sing, everything falls apart. If she can't sing, how will he get James back?

"I mean I can't sing," she says. "When I try, when I even think about trying, my voice gets all strangled."

"Maybe you're fatigued from being in the studio and recording your album."

"I haven't been in the studio for three weeks," she replies.

"But the photos . . ." Not one week ago, he and James had seen photos of her accompanied by updates about how well everything was going.

"They were taken before," she says. "Posted to keep up the facade. Until I got my voice back."

"But you will get it back? And finish?"

She shakes her head. "Maybe not."

Harun imagines James finding out about Freya and the

incomplete album, and though he only just met her and clearly has nothing to do with it, it feels like his fault, somehow.

Tears spring to his eyes. As a child he wept so often that his older brothers teased him and Ammi scolded him. "Why do you cry so much? Not even your sister cries so much." Without anyone telling him, he knew the tears carried his secret the way blood carries DNA. He learned not to cry. Even with James, he did not cry. Not even when James did and he thought it would kill him.

"Hey," Freya says, wiping her own tears. She puts her hand on his, and Nathaniel puts his on top of Freya's, and Harun savors the weight of it like he would a heavy blanket on a cold night. "It's not your problem. You don't have to worry about it."

But she's wrong. She might not be his solution, but this *is* his problem.

"But James loves you. He's your biggest fan."

Freya smiles sadly. Nathaniel finishes chewing the rest of his second grilled cheese sandwich.

"Who's James?" Nathaniel asks.

"He's my . . ." Harun begins.

What Harun should say is that James is his ex-boyfriend. Because as of last week (*Get the fuck out my life*), that's what he is. But Harun has never once claimed James as his *boyfriend*. He's never told anyone about this boy he has been in love with for the past eighteen months. Even when he'd told his cousin, he hadn't said the word *boyfriend*. He'd never said James's name. And it doesn't seem fair to say he's his ex-boyfriend when he never even got to claim him.

"My boyfriend," Harun says. "And he's totally obsessed with you. But not in a creepy way."

"Oh yeah?" Freya sounds amused.

"Yeah." And it's like he's been uncorked, and out flow all the things he has never been able to tell anyone about James. About how James believes in the best in everyone, and how he hates the cold, and how he claims he can take any five ingredients and cook them into something delicious (a feat Harun has never actually seen performed, though he has tasted the evidence of it, the plastic containers full of stews and pastas James has cooked for him). And how when he was young, their apartment came with a shower curtain that was a map of the world, and how he used up all the hot water memorizing all the countries, even ones that no longer existed (like Yugoslavia), and how even though he's never left the tri-state area, he has the most powerful wanderlust. How on the cold days, he and Harun pretend they're traveling to the faraway places.

And he tells Freya about James's devotion to her, careful to temper his fandom the way James himself once had. "There's something you should know about me," he'd told Harun, and Harun had steeled himself for some kind of deal breaker (*I have a boyfriend, I am a space alien*), but instead James had confessed that he had a kind of strange obsession with a singer. He told Harun how he had come across the Sisters K covering "I Will Survive" the very day his father kicked him out of the house, and felt as though Freya were singing directly to him. And he wrote to her. And she replied.

— — —

There have been thousands of comments. But Freya remembers that one. She remembers writing back to that boy. She remembers reading his note and thinking of the night she realized her father wasn't coming back, thinking she wouldn't survive. She had, and so would he.

She looks at Harun, at Nathaniel. Unlike her mother, or Hayden, she does not believe in anything resembling destiny. But at that moment, it's hard not to believe that the three of them were meant to meet.

THE ORDER OF LOSS
PART VII

FREYA

Hayden hadn't called us back for six months.

Mom tried to remain positive. Because she now read everything about him, she knew he was in the studio with Mélange and after that on tour with Lulia. "When he's working with an artist, he's completely immersed," Mom declared. "When it's your turn to be in the studio with him, you'll be glad about that."

"Not gonna happen," Sabrina said with her usual certainty.

I nodded and pretended to agree. But though my sister was usually right, I could sense unfinished business. I kept hearing his question. *Are you hungry enough?* he'd asked *me* this question. I hadn't answered. But at some point, whether it was to Hayden or someone else, I knew I'd have to.

We went back to doing what we'd been doing: weekly video drops of new songs, daily photo posts. Mom storyboarded things out weeks in advance. Our numbers continued to climb. If Mom's optimism wavered, she didn't let it show.

"He'll call," she said.

When, finally, his office did call, requesting a second meeting for the very next day, Mom was triumphant, as if Hayden had been on the verge of discarding us but she'd mentally dreamed us back into contention.

"He asked for much more this time," she said, reading through the notes she'd taken. "He wants analytics across platforms. Accounting of all endorsement offers, licensing. Oh, and he wants to hear something new from you. An original song, not yet posted."

"We don't have anything ready," Sabrina said. "We can't just pull a brand-new song out of our asses."

"What about 'The Space Between'?" Mom asked. That was a song we'd been working on. Mom went back to her notes. "Let's see. His assistant says he wants to hear something unique and . . ." Mom shuffled through her notes to get the words exactly right. "All his own."

All his own. A warning right there.

"I guess we'll have to do 'The Space Between,'" Sabrina said, sounding defeated. "He might've given us more time."

"Actually," I began, "I have something else."

"No you don't," Sabrina snapped. That was Sabrina through and through. If she didn't see it, it didn't exist.

Mom looked at me. When I didn't say anything, she said, "If you've got something in the works, let's hear it."

"Yes," Sabrina said scathingly. "Let's hear it."

"Actually, you already have," I told Sabrina.

"What?"

"'Little White Dress'? The one you called 'a pathetic piece of sentimental crap.'" I pulled out my phone and opened the audio file.

Sabrina's normally impassive face flashed with so many emotions at once: anger and disgust and hurt. "You *recorded* that? Without me?"

"Not the whole thing . . ." I stammered. "Just some vocal and percussion of the chorus and the bridge. Because I thought if you heard—"

She cut me off with a flick of her hand. "There's nothing that will make me change my mind about that song."

I was used to Sabrina's strong opinions and her veto power, but something about her high-handedness pissed me off. And that was before she said: "Look. I'm the only one who'll be honest with you. And the truth is, you're a weak songwriter. Your stuff is so sentimental, so young. It makes you sound like an amateur."

"I'm seventeen! And last time I checked, we were both amateurs."

"Isn't the idea for us to take it to the next level? Well, not with that song we won't."

"Why are you acting so—"

"Jealous?" she interrupted. She barked out a laugh. "Jealous of you?"

Controlling was what I was going to say. But *jealous* worked too.

"Let's just take a beat." Mom turned to Sabrina. "Can we at least hear it?" Even when it was my song, it was still the two of them. It would always be the two of them.

Sabrina slumped back without raising any more objections. She glared as if daring me to touch my finger to the play button.

I hit play.

All that I said I wanted
Was a little white, little white dress
All that I said I needed
Was a little white, little white dress—Oh,
Do you remember? We used to sing:
Eshururururu, eshururururu
Eshururururu, hushabye, hushabye, hushabye

There were two more verses, but with Sabrina glowering, I couldn't bear to play them. I turned off the recording. "You get the idea," I told Mom.

Mom looked astonished, as if she didn't quite recognize the song or the person singing. "Well," she said. "It's certainly different."

"It's not arranged, but I was going for a more stripped-down sound," I said. "Maybe just percussion and some piano."

"It is unique," Mom said, "with the Ethiopian melodies in there. I imagine Hayden hasn't heard anything like that."

She was warming to the song. I could tell. So could Sabrina. She put her foot down. "I'm not singing that."

"Honey," Mom said. "Let's be professional about this."

"Professional? How is airing Freya's daddy issues in front of Hayden Booth professional?"

"What are you talking about?" I yelled.

"It's been seven years," she said, tapping her chest. "Get over it."

"*You* get over it!" I shouted.

"Maybe I will. Maybe I'm tired of taking care of you."

"That's what you call it? Because I'd call it undermining me. Or back-drafting off me."

When I got angry, I boiled. When Sabrina got mad, she froze. It was one of the millions of things that differentiated us. But at that moment, the weather changed. Sabrina blazed with a fury that set the whole room on fire, before it sucked in on itself and her face went blank, her voice went icy.

"If you sing that song," she told me, "you sing it alone."

— — —

We agreed to sing "The Space Between" and practiced all night without actually speaking. We were still not speaking when we drove down to Hayden's offices the next day. But the minute the elevator doors opened, my anger evaporated and I was left with a weirdly homesick feeling. I wanted to take it all back. To sing as we had that night in bed or to clasp hands as we'd done last time we'd faced Hayden. But Sabrina stood with her arms rigid, her fists balled, her face statue-still.

Mom checked in with the assistant. Sabrina and I sat down.

"Sabrina," I whispered. "About 'Little White Dress' . . ."

"Don't!" she hissed. She swiveled around to me, her eyes hard little kernels, and opened her mouth to continue, but at that moment Hayden's assistant called her name. She stood up. I stood too.

"He wants you separately this time," the assistant said.

A feeling of dread came over me. It was like watching the girl in the horror movie descending the stairs into the basement alone. You wanted to yell, but even if you did, she never listened.

Sabrina went into the office, and I sat down next to Mom, my knees bobbing up, down, up, down. Mom put her hand on them, but it didn't help. Through the door I heard Sabrina sing "The Space Between," the song we were meant to sing together. After she finished, she stayed in a long time, the low tones of their murmured conversation impossible to decipher. Mom started to look nervous. "Wonder what they're talking about?" she said, staring endlessly at her phone, as if Sabrina was going to mentally text her the news.

I told myself Hayden was giving her another lecture about fame. I told myself Hayden was asking her about our videos, or our brand strategy, or inquiring where she saw herself in ten years.

But I couldn't shake the bad feeling that we'd walked into this building as the Sisters K but were going to leave as something else.

I heard Sabrina singing again. But not "The Space Between" or any of the other songs we'd written together. She was singing "Tschay Hailu." The song my father sang to me. The first song we'd ever sung together.

And that's when I knew. She'd betrayed me.

4

YOU MUST DO THINGS THE PROPER WAY

When they leave the diner, something's different. None of them can say what. But Nathaniel knows he's heard Freya's song before, even though he's never watched a YouTube music video in his life. And Freya remembers Harun's boyfriend, even though she gets hundreds of thousands of comments. And Harun is here today, with Freya, even though she is Freya.

— — —

As they walk aimlessly, Nathaniel asks shy questions about what happened to Freya's voice.

She has asked herself the same questions, but she still can't explain the loss. She tells Nathaniel and Harun about the day before it all went sideways, how she'd sung hard, too hard, pushed herself past her boundaries, so when she came in the next morning, unable to sing, everyone thought it was strain. She was given the morning off and a massage courtesy of Hayden's personal masseuse. But that afternoon it was even worse, and the next day worse yet. And she knew it wasn't a strain—that, she would feel. This was an absence. This was the thing she'd always done, always known how to do, vacating her, like a soul leaving a body after death. "Don't overthink it," her mother advised her, but that assumed Freya had ever thought about how to sing in the first place. She'd sung her first note when she was one minute old. Singing was something she'd done as automatically as breathing. And suddenly she couldn't sing. Some days, she could barely breathe.

"When did all this happen?" Harun asks.

Freya sighs. A million years ago. That's what it seems like for how tired it makes her. "Three weeks ago."

"Three weeks!" Harun exclaims. "That's nothing. Can't they wait for you?"

"They can, but they won't," Freya says. "After the doctor this morning, Hayden called me to his office. I'm pretty sure it was to let me go. Which is why *I* didn't go. He can't fire me if I'm not there."

"But it's only been three weeks," Harun repeats. He seems very caught up on that. He doesn't know that Hayden's time is measured in gold, and three lost weeks is a bill none of them can pay.

"I've lost my slot," Freya explains. "In two weeks he goes into the studio with Lulia."

"Can't you record after Julia?" Nathaniel says.

"Lulia," Harun corrects.

"Lulia, then."

"It doesn't work like that." Freya is tired of talking about this, tired of trying to divine how the mind of Hayden Booth works. What will please him. What will piss him off. What counts as loyalty and what as betrayal. She knows, in her bones, he's going to dump her. Her mother doesn't believe this. Why would someone spend two years investing in something only to toss it aside? It's bad business. But Freya knows that in spite of his proclamation that art is personal and business is not, with Hayden, everything is business and everything is personal.

"It's like he's become legendary for his ability to launch artists," she says to Harun and Nathaniel. "He has a formula, and it works. It's always worked. It's why he's so picky about who he chooses to work with. They have to have very specific qualities."

Like talent. And It factor. And hunger. That might be Hayden's true superhuman strength: being able to smell who is hungry enough to do what it takes, to sacrifice things like privacy, autonomy . . . family.

But she doesn't tell Harun and Nathaniel that. Instead, she tells them about the third meeting with Hayden, the first one after Sabrina had been cut loose, when it was just Freya and her mother. He'd laid out his entire plan. They'd need two years, he said. The Sisters K were known, but Freya was not. They needed to convert the Sisters K fans to Freya fans, and to bring many more new fans into the fold. They would build her profile across all platforms, select appearances where she'd garner a lot of coverage, get her used to performing in front of a crowd, increase her Q factor, grow her into a household name. Then they could drop the first single. After that, they would pull back a bit, build more mystery into it, more hunger. Only then would they go into the studio. When the album came out, Hayden predicted, its success, like Lulia's and Mélange's before her, would be inevitable.

Freya's mom had been panting at all this, but Freya herself was uneasy. It seemed like a lot of dominoes had to fall just right. What if things didn't work that way?

Hayden seemed bemused by her skepticism. And then he launched into one of his lectures. "You think people like art, like music because of *personal taste*?" he'd said, scoffing at the idea of something so individual. "It's nothing but positioning, love. You frame things a certain way. This is hot. This is edgy. This is the next big thing that you'll want to know about first. You do that right and you barely have to do anything else. Your product doesn't even have to be that good if you frame it right." He shook his head, smiling, about how easy it all was. "People are moths, drawn to light. Our job is to make you the brightest light."

"Maybe that's what's pissed him off," Freya tells Nathaniel and Harun now. "Not so much that I'm having problems with my voice, but that I disrupted his march toward inevitability." For a brief moment, this insight allows her to feel almost sympathetic toward Hayden. Star-making is the thing he's always done as naturally as breathing, and Freya went and fucked it up. "In his eyes, it was a betrayal."

"If anyone is betrayed in this scenario, it is you," Harun says.

Freya knows full well that isn't true, but she appreciates him for saying so.

"He shouldn't get to fire you," Harun continues, his voice clipped and urgent. "You need more time. He should give you more time. People need to be patient with other people. To understand that sometimes things don't happen on a schedule, that certain things can't be rushed. That when you pressure someone, mistakes occur."

Harun speaks with such vehemence, as if this matters deeply to him. As if he's insulted by Hayden's behavior. Freya is touched, but that changes nothing.

Hayden swings his power like a sledgehammer. He can do what he wants; if you want to be in his universe—and they all do—you take it. On the rare occasions Freya's mother ever dares to say anything negative about Hayden, she does it in a whisper, even if the two of them are alone in the apartment.

"You should go make your case," Harun urges. "Tell him to give you more time. You need to do this."

She looks to Nathaniel, who hasn't commented on any of this. "What do you think?"

"What happens if he fires you?" Nathaniel asks.

Your numbers will drop. Your fans will forget you.

"I lose everything," Freya says.

— — —

Nathaniel knows what it means to lose everything. It really means losing yourself. It is the worst thing that can happen.

He would do anything to keep this from happening to another person.

"What can I do?" he asks.

— — —

"What can *we* do?" Harun corrects. He doesn't know what it means to lose everything, but he suspects he's dangerously close to finding out.

— — —

Their enthusiasm—their righteous anger—is infectious. It makes Freya want to do something she has never been able to do: speak for herself.

Only that would mean facing Hayden alone. Bad things happen when she's alone with him.

But maybe she doesn't have to be alone.

"Will you guys come with me?" she asks in a small voice. "To confront him?"

She's only just met them. They don't know what she intends to do. She doesn't know what she intends to do. She's flying blind. They must see it.

But they don't hesitate. "Yes," they reply.

— — —

When they arrive at Hayden's SoHo offices, Freya feels like puking.

"I feel like puking," she says.

"Feel free to do it on my shoes," Nathaniel offers.

This is funny, but she doesn't laugh, because she really does feel like puking, and it's better not to tempt fate.

They ride the elevator up to Hayden's office. Freya's knees begin to buckle as she realizes she's about to face Hayden with no idea of what to say. During media training, she'd been taught to draw up three talking points before every interview, and no matter what the interviewer asked, to respond with her talking points. It was when people diverged that they ran into trouble, said things they couldn't take back.

But here she is, in the elevator up to Hayden's office, and she hasn't even figured out what she should say. Which is an amateur move; you don't take on Hayden Booth with no strategic planning, a lesson Freya should've learned.

She's going to faint.

The elevator door opens. Freya has a sudden body memory of the first time she and Sabrina came here, how when the doors had opened, they'd reached for each other's hand. She can still feel Sabrina's grip—is certain that if she looks down, the half moons of her sister's nails will be there.

She looks. They aren't.

This was a dumb idea. There's nothing she can do or say that will change anything. But then Nathaniel puts his hand on the small of her back and Harun makes an after-you gesture, holding the elevator door open, and she is whisked into Hayden's lobby, and before she can change her mind, the elevator door closes behind her.

The lobby is full of enormous framed photos of Hayden, that crooked grin of his as he mugs for the camera with,

well, everyone who matters in the world of pop music. Seeing them, Harun gasps. Which is precisely the point.

One of Hayden's interchangeable assistants—intimidatingly
beautiful, headset attached like a cyborg—looks up from the
desk. "Freya," the assistant says coolly. "We were expecting
you earlier."

"I wasn't available earlier," Freya says, attempting to
recreate the Freya of the narrative, the one who's tough as
nails, as ruthless as the man who discovered her (just ask
Sabrina). The Freya who is not intimidated by an assistant.
"Is Hayden in?"

"He's not available," the assistant says.

"Is he here?"

"No."

"Is he gone for the day?" It's after five, but Hayden often
stayed late at the office.

"No, but it'll be a while."

What else is new?

"We'll wait," Harun announces.

Freya wants to tell Harun they could be here for hours.
Hayden enjoys making people wait almost as much as he
hates waiting.

But Harun's already sat down on the leather couch.
Nathaniel has sat down next to him. They've left a square
between them for her. Freya sits and stares at Hayden's office door. Gunmetal gray with a bright, shiny knob. He could
be in there. He could be punishing her or fucking with her
or being Hayden. The first time, he'd made them wait two

hours. The assistants had offered no explanation, no apology, not even water.

"Would you like some water?" the assistant asks, and Freya feels momentarily better that if nothing else, she is now (still) a person who is offered water upon arrival.

Only the stupid assistant isn't even asking her. She's asking Nathaniel.

"Sure," Nathaniel says.

"Still or sparkling?"

The assistant is fawning, like Nathaniel is someone almost-famous, and Freya understands it's because he's good-looking enough to be someone famous, and those kinds of looks—in New York City, anyhow—are a self-fulfilling prophecy.

"Huh?" Nathaniel says.

"Bubbles or no bubbles?" the assistant says.

"Uhh, bubbles, I guess."

"Two shakes," the assistant replies without asking if Freya or Harun want water, let alone still or sparkling.

The creep of jealousy comes on strong and fast and surprising. Freya isn't jealous because Nathaniel is offered water. She's jealous because that bitch is flirting with him. And he belongs to her. *She's* his emergency contact. And that's when Freya realizes she no longer simply feels responsible for Nathaniel. She likes him. The fluttery feeling in her stomach cannot be fully attributed to the prospect of facing Hayden.

It's been so long since she liked a guy, or allowed herself to. Not since Tai. They'd been set up a while ago, two up-and-comers whose combined star power could generate some heat. They played the couple, made a minor splash, got in a few of the tabloids, which was the plan, and she actually liked him, which wasn't.

They'd slept together in a two-thousand-dollar-a-night hotel suite they'd been given for free in exchange for a post from an "it couple" about its new rooftop bar. The next morning she woke up to find him FaceTiming his boyfriend. The boyfriend waved at Freya. "Don't worry," Tai said. "We're fluid and open." When Freya had gotten upset, he'd been confused. "But we had fun, right? And this suite is sweet. Should we take a selfie on the balcony before we go?" She'd agreed. The shot was still reposted, fans still shipping Freya and Tai.

The assistant returns with a bottle of Pellegrino and one glass.

One glass. Seriously? Freya clears her throat.

"Oh, sorry. Did you want some water too?" the assistant asks.

Freya would prefer to take the contoured bottle and shove it up her—

"Yes," Harun says. "No bubbles."

"Same," Freya says.

"Okay. Be right back." She flashes a smile at Nathaniel. "Holler if you need anything else."

Nathaniel seems flummoxed by the attention, and Freya sees he doesn't even know he's being flirted with. The city is full of people who overvalue their talent, their looks, their charisma. Someone like Nathaniel is a purple unicorn.

"I'm all good," he tells the assistant.

Freya stares at the office door, closed, like it was that day.

Betrayals rarely take place out in the open. She's been in there so many times she can draw the landscape in her mind: his desk, marble, heavy, expensive, and cold. The framed records on the wall. The photos of him alongside a veritable who's who of pop music: Lulia and Rufus Q, who are his protégés, and other famous artists and producers, him and Kanye and Kim, him and Jay and Bey and Bono and Bowie and others whom he counted as friends, or, more to the point, could display as friends. The framed graffiti print. The computer covered in sticky notes, because—and Freya always found this a little hilarious—for all Hayden's genius when it comes to manipulating social media, he's a technophobe who doesn't know how to use his computer.

On that computer is a file folder with her name on it. The first time she'd seen the file, she'd felt a wave of euphoria, the same way she had the first time their video had gone viral or their first YouTube video had passed a million views. A moment of relief. She had nearly reached the finish line, after which everything would be okay. She hadn't known what was in the file, only that it was somehow proof.

She now knows what's in the file: basically everything. Hayden has assistants cull every bit of press, every social media hit, every tagged post. Plus all her analytics, her contracts, her emails (or her mother's), and the vestiges of her voice in all the recordings he has. As for the finish line, either she's no closer or it keeps moving.

She jumps up, knowing suddenly and for the first time in a long time exactly what she wants to do. "Nathaniel," she whispers, "I need you to flirt with the assistant."

"What?"

"Flirt."

"Me? How?"

"Bat your eyes. Be yourself. She already likes you. Just tell her we had to leave, and flirt so she forgets to ask any questions." She turns to Harun. "Is your boyfriend really my biggest fan?"

She sees Harun hesitate, a fault line crack across his face, but just as quickly he rights himself. "Yes," he says, tentatively at first. Then more forcefully: "He is."

She's in full-on diva mode, but for once it's not an act. She knows exactly what she wants to do.

"Then he'd want you to do this. Come on."

— — —

The assistant returns with two more waters. She looks around. "Where'd they go?" she asks Nathaniel.

Nathaniel freezes. Freya instructed him to flirt. He doesn't know how to flirt. He once did. He must have. He remembers girls, girlfriends, but that was such a long time ago, before he'd turned feral. But he will flirt because Freya told him to, and if she told him to do a handstand and quack like a duck, he'd do that too.

"They left," he tells the assistant, and for good measure, he bats his eyelashes. "But I'm still here."

She smiles at him. Licks her lips. "So you are."

Maybe he does know how to flirt.

— — —

Freya is going to delete herself from Hayden's computer. It's a symbolic move. She gets that. But it's necessary just the same. Hayden will get it. She can't lose a race she refuses to run. He can't fire her if she quits.

She goes straight to the computer. She clicks on the mouse and the monitor lights up. There's no lock to it because one time Hayden forgot the code and it took a whole twenty minutes to locate an assistant, and wasting twenty minutes of Hayden's time is a sin.

His schedule is up on the screen. The block of weeks earlier in the month have her name on every day and most other appointments blocked out—her mother had been right about the devotion he gives to his artists, so long as they're behaving— but the past two weeks have been updated, the holes she left in the schedule easily replaced. In two weeks, after his week on the private island, it's Lulia's name that blocks out the schedule. Freya is certain Lulia will take her entire six weeks. She will leave no holes.

First, Freya deletes herself from the calendar. She deletes the recording session. She deletes today's doctor's appointment. She deletes it all.

"What are you doing?" Harun asks.

"Nothing. Just let me know if the assistant is coming, and be quiet!" she whispers.

Freya closes the calendar. Hayden's desktop picture is Lulia, of course. It's almost like he knew Freya was coming and set-designed the office to mess with her head. On the desktop are several folders, each labeled with the name of the artists he works with: Lulia, Mélange, Rufus Q, and Freya.

She clicks open her folder. Inside is everything. Everything she gave Hayden. And everything he took.

— — —

"You look familiar. Are you a model?" the assistant asks Nathaniel. "An actor?"

"Umm, no?"

"You could be."

"Uhh, thanks?" And because he's meant to be flirting, he smiles what he thinks is maybe the coquettish grin of an actor or model.

"I could take some headshots for you if you like. It's what I do, photography. This"—she gestures to her desk—"is temporary."

"Most things are," Nathaniel says.

She laughs at that. Nathaniel laughs too, though it wasn't a joke.

"I love your eyes," she says. "How'd they get like that?"

Nathaniel has never told anyone the story before, but for a moment he imagines what it would be like to explain what really happened—not just how he lost his eye, but why. What it's been like to exist in that house on the edge of the forest with his father. The fellowship of two. He glances toward the office, where Harun and Freya are. He imagines telling them. He looks back at the assistant. "Heterochromia," he lies. "Genetic condition."

— — —

"What are you doing?" Harun asks, peering over Freya's shoulder at the monitor.

"I'm erasing myself before he can erase me."

"You're what?"

"I'm deleting all my files. Except for one."

"Which one?"

He looks at the screen as Freya scrolls through hundreds of files: PDFs, JPEGs, videos.

"A master."

"What's a master?"

"The original recordings, before a song is mixed."

"Why do you want them?"

"Not them. Just one."

"Why?"

"Because it belongs to me."

She keeps scrolling until she finds it. *Little White Dress.ptx*. Bingo.

"Do you know the best way to transfer a file and completely erase it?" she asks Harun.

"Yes, but isn't that stealing?"

"Technically, it's more like hacking."

"If it's yours, why can't you just ask for it back?"

"It doesn't work like that. Hayden owns the masters. He

owns the copyrights. He owns everything." This was the deal they'd signed. She remembers sitting in that big conference room: Freya, her mother, Hayden, the team of lawyers. They were the label's lawyers. Hayden's lawyers. "Shouldn't we have a lawyer?" Freya had asked her mother. "We are your lawyers," Hayden's attorneys had told them. "We creative types have to stick together," Hayden had said.

Freya glances at the print on the wall. *Art is personal. Business is not.* It wasn't like he didn't warn them.

The rest of the songs, he can have, use for whatever he wants, sell them for scrap, repurpose them for the next shiny girl. But not this song. This song is hers.

She opens her mail program and attempts to attach the file. Harun watches her, not saying a thing.

— — —

Harun is a coward. How many times does he have to say this? He's the kind of coward who shatters hearts. The kind of coward who allows his family to participate in an enormous hoax. The kind of coward who does not casually break and enter the offices of powerful men like Hayden Booth.

He wants to help Freya in any way he can, but even that is for cowardly reasons. To get James back. That's why he said yes to all this.

But stealing? Harun is a good boy. When Saif was rebelling, not going to mosque, Harun still went. When Saif was making Ammi cry by marrying a white girl, Harun was doing his best not to make Ammi cry. Because he's a good son.

But here he is, possibly participating in a crime. What if he gets arrested? What would people think? What would his parents say? Would they still love him?

— — —

The file is too big. It won't let her email it. Freya knows you're supposed to compress the file or something, but she doesn't remember how.

Harun is just staring at her.

"Are you going to help me or not?" she asks.

— — —

Harun pictures Abu coming to the police station to fetch him, the felony arrest on his record. The shame in his father's eyes.

Though if he got arrested, he wouldn't be able to leave tomorrow. He'd have an excuse not to get on that plane.

As mentioned, a coward.

— — —

Freya is growing frustrated. She tries to attach the file to an email again. When it doesn't work, she smacks the machine.

"Shit," she says.

— — —

Harun watches Freya, knowing it won't work; the file is too large, and anyway, there will be a copy in the sent folder, and even if she thinks to delete that, the digital footprint will remain on the server.

His insides are itchy with frustration and impatience, and seeing Freya's expression, he understands that he's feeling exactly as she is. He's feeling it on behalf of her, as if for one moment he has stepped out of his own problems and into someone else's, and frankly, it's a relief. Particularly when this is a problem he can solve.

Freya tries once again to attach the enormous file. This time, Harun steps between her and the computer.

"You must do things the proper way," he says, pulling out his keychain, which contains his house keys, his school ID fob, and the small flash drive he purchased expressly to store photographs, texts, and emails from James in a safe place. But he never did. He was too scared he'd be found out, so the drive remains empty.

He inserts the drive into the port. The sound of laughter—Nathaniel's laughter, intermingled with the assistant's—flutes out from the lobby through the closed door.

"Sounds like he's flirting well," Harun says.

Freya frowns, and Harun feels bad. Now that he has stepped out of himself for five seconds, he realizes something has been crackling between those two all day. "Don't worry," Harun adds. "He likes you too."

"You think?" Freya asks, and the yearning in her eyes is so familiar, he's no longer sure if it's her yearning or his pumping through his veins.

A phone rings: Hayden's office extension, as well as the assistant's desk. Freya glances at the caller ID.

"It's Hayden's cell," she whispers.

"If the assistant doesn't know we're here, neither does he," Harun says, suddenly full of smooth confidence.

"I wouldn't count on that. Hayden sees everything," she says.

"No one sees everything." He pauses for a minute. "Except maybe God."

"Hayden is God." The line on the phone blinks. "Hurry."

— — —

While the assistant is on the phone, Nathaniel hears her mention Freya. "Been and gone." She looks at Nathaniel a little suspiciously, and he lets loose his brightest smile yet.

"No, she didn't say what she wanted." A pause. "She left without waiting. I don't control her." A defensive whine in her voice. "All right, all right. I'll get her back." She hangs up the phone and peers up at Nathaniel, not smiling anymore.

"Where did Freya go?" she asks him.

He may be a bad flirt, but he's an expert liar. "Not sure." He pulls out his phone. "Let me call her." He excuses himself to the waiting area and calls the only number stored in his phone.

"Tell me something good," his dad says.

"Hey, it's me," he says. He speaks to the void, as he's done so often these past few weeks. Only it doesn't feel like the ghost of his father he's talking to. Because in his mind, he's talking to Freya and Harun.

— — —

"How much longer?" Freya asks.

"Not long. Transferring the file."

Freya watches the progress, itchy with suspense: 10 percent, 18 percent.

26 percent.

Her hearts starts to speed up.

43 percent.

"Hurry," she says to the heedless computer.

The office phone line goes dark, then lights up again.

68 percent.

"Come on," she urges.

"It's a computer," Harun says. "It can't understand you."

The computer ticks to 73 percent and just stops.

"What happened?" Freya asks. "Is it stuck?"

"It's not stuck. It's just processing," Harun says.

"Make it process faster," Freya cries, giving the computer a good whack.

"You must do things the proper way," he says again.

The monitor ticks to 80 percent.

"I'm tired of the proper way," she says.

93 and 100. Freya lunges for the flash drive.

He stops her and ejects the drive and replaces the cap and puts the drive back on his keychain. Freya drags the files to the trash.

"Not that way," he says. Harun opens the file, and instead of dragging it to the trash, he deletes the contents and leaves the file name intact. He does a search for files with the same name and does the same with a version saved in the cloud. Freya sees the name of the file show up in the finder.

"I thought you deleted it," Freya says.

"I did. This is a ghost file. I deleted the actual contents but left just the folder there." Harun smiles. "To avoid suspicion."

Freya is in a hurry, but she takes a few seconds to appraise Harun. "You're kind of devious, aren't you?"

Harun allows the smallest of smiles. "You have no idea."

— — —

Nathaniel is still talking to Freya on the phone when she and Harun emerge from the office, laughing, victorious.

"What the . . . ?" the assistant asks.

"Oh, there you are," Nathaniel says, hanging up his phone.

"What were you doing in there?" the assistant demands.

Freya doesn't answer. She takes Nathaniel's hand. "Gotta go," she trills.

"Did you know they were in there?" the assistant asks Nathaniel. She turns to Freya. "Hayden's not going to be happy about that."

"Oh well," Freya says, taking Harun's hand and leading them all to the elevator bank.

"What should I tell Hayden?" the assistant asks.

Harun presses the elevator button. Just as the elevator

yawns opens, Freya turns to the assistant. "Tell him that art is personal. Business is not." And the door closes. The three of them descend, holding hands, each one of them experiencing something that only hours before seemed inconceivable: happiness.

5

HAPPINESS

They keep running until they're several blocks from Hayden's office, not because they think they're being pursued but because even with a possible concussion and a cut-up heel, it feels ridiculously good to be sprinting down the street, holding hands, a chain of three, laughing as they send irritated pedestrians skittering out of their way like pigeons.

They cut right, through a park—if you can call a handful of benches and a baseball diamond a park—when Nathaniel suddenly skids to a halt, nose twitching like he smells the pickup softball game. The teams are warming up, he can tell. The pitcher lets loose a drop ball, and the batter pops a wide foul, the ball sailing in their direction. On instinct, Nathaniel's left arm shoots up, his mind's eye seeing the catch before it happens. The smack of the leather against his palm sounds like a kiss.

It's only when he looks down that he realizes he caught a foul in someone else's game. "Sorry," he calls, staring at the ball in his hand in wonder, unable to believe he caught it. But he did. And the pitcher is waiting, so, sense memory taking over once again, he throws it with aim so perfect the pitcher only needs to lift his glove to complete the catch.

"Thanks," the pitcher calls, jogging over to where the three of them stand. "You play?" he asks Nathaniel.

"Used to."

"Cool, cool. See those guys over there?" He gestures with his chin to a group of players standing on the edge of the field. They're older, dressed in impeccably crisp pinstripe jerseys, as opposed to the teams playing, twentysomethings wearing street clothes. "They're from the Lawyers League. They're vulturing us because we're down a few and you're not supposed to hold the field without a full roster, but we *have* a full roster, just a bunch of our guys are late." He sticks out his right hand and taps his chest with his gloved hand. "I'm Finny, by the way."

Nathaniel shakes and introduces himself, Freya, and Harun. "How many are you down?"

"Three on our side, all stuck on the same stalled subway. Fucking MTA." Finny shakes his head. "We're playing with a couple of guys down in the outfield, but they're breathing down our necks." He glances at Nathaniel, Harun, and Freya. "There are three of you. You want to step in until my players can get here?"

Nathaniel has not played ball, has not wanted to play ball, since that day, nearly four years ago, when his coach invited him for a game of catch. But today he wants to play.

"Yeah!" Nathaniel says emphatically.

"No!" Freya and Harun say equally emphatically.

Nathaniel doesn't want to be pushy. But man, he wants in on the game. His hand is still tingling from that catch.

"And you shouldn't be playing either," Harun adds. "The doctor said no excessive physical activity."

"I feel fine," Nathaniel says. "Better than I have in ages. And you both said the doctor was incompetent."

"So you play," Harun says.

"Not if you don't."

"I don't play softball. I play cricket," Harun says.

"What position?" Nathaniel asks.

"Wicket-keeper."

"Not so different from catcher, right?" Nathaniel turns to Finny. "You need a catcher?"

"We'll take what we can get. We play for beers, so the stakes are incredibly low. Also, you get beer whether you win or lose."

"How do you know about cricket?" Harun asks Nathaniel. "Americans never know about cricket."

"I watched a documentary about a team from Afghanistan."

"You've seen *Out of the Ashes*?" Harun asks. "I loved that movie."

Nathaniel nods. "And also the one about the West Indian team. My father went through a cricket obsession. Called it the only gentleman's sport."

— — —

Harun's father has said the same thing. He often said that cricket taught the rules of civility. "Without that, society comes apart."

Harun tried to teach James the rules once, on a particularly nasty February day, but James wasn't having any part of it. Not even after Harun showed him photos of Shahid Afridi, not even after he showed him pictures of a young Imran Khan.

Harun does not want to play softball. But Nathaniel knows about cricket. He imagines Nathaniel's father and his own having a conversation about this over tea.

"The problem is, I don't actually know how to play beyond what I learned in elementary school," Harun admits.

"No worries. We'll plug you in as catcher," Finny says. "Just catch the ball and throw it to me."

Harun stands the chance of being humiliated, or laughed at, or making a total hash of it. But Nathaniel hasn't asked for one thing this whole day. And it felt so good to do something for Freya before. Cowardice and selfishness get so very tiresome.

"Look, we really don't care if you do anything," Finny says. "We just need bodies on the field till our guys arrive."

Harun turns to Freya. It's all or nothing. He's not sure when it became that. But it has.

— — —

"Oh no," Freya says. "Don't look at me. I don't play sports. I play music."

Played music.

"I'm not doing it if you don't," Nathaniel says.

"We'll stick you in center field," Finny tells Nathaniel. "You in right field," he tells Freya. "He'll cover for you."

"But I don't have a . . . what's it called? Glove?"

"We've got gear."

"But I'm left-handed," Freya says, the softball version of a Hail Mary pass. "Don't I need a different glove?"

"We've got left-handed gloves."

Nathaniel, Harun, and Finny all look at Freya, a triple whammy of puppy-dog eyes. "That's not fair," Freya says, "to put that much pressure on me." But she's smiling.

"I did just commit a crime for you," Harun says.

"And I flirted with that awful assistant for you," Nathaniel says.

"And hey, I just met you, but you'd be doing me a solid," Finny says.

"So the assistant was awful, was she?" Freya asks Nathaniel, utterly embarrassed by how much this snipe pleases her.

"Wasn't her fault," Nathaniel says. "She just wasn't you."

And that does it. Freya's a goner. She'd go skydiving if he asked, and she's terrified of heights. Moments later, she's unrecognizable in someone's battered lefty glove and someone else's baseball cap. Standing in right field, she wonders: *How did I get here?* Only she's not thinking about the ball field, specifically, but here with Harun and Nathaniel. Also the ball field. She's never played softball in her life.

How did I get here? she asks herself again. But the answer doesn't matter. What matters is that she did.

— — —

As Harun squats behind home plate, his phone buzzes with a text. The dinner in his honor is not due to start for a while yet, but Ammi always gets nervous if you're not at least a half hour early.

He can picture his family sitting around the dining room table, the extra leaf added to make room for all of them and all the dishes Ammi has been preparing. Ammi will pace. She won't stop until they're all seated and eating. The longer his absence goes, the faster she will pace. She will check the clock over the mantel, she will wring her hands. *"Fikar nahi karo,"* Abu will tell her. "Don't worry." The trains are late, the traffic is heavy, children lose track of themselves. It will go on like this until too much time passes for these excuses to be believable, and even Abu's face will begin to furrow with worry.

"We're a full roster now," Finny is telling the glaring lawyers in pinstripes. "So step the hell off. This field is ours until seven."

Harun's phone buzzes again. Finny lopes back to the pitcher's mound. "You ready?" he calls to Harun.

"No."

Finny grins. "Batter up."

— — —

"You know I have no idea what I'm doing?" Freya tells Nathaniel from the safe recesses of the outfield.

"I got you covered," Nathaniel says.

Freya knows he's talking about baseball, but she feels warm all over. "I'm holding you to that."

— — —

Nathaniel's having a blast. He can't remember the last time he's had such fun. The smell of the grass, the soil, the particular sound a ball makes connecting with a bat. It brings something back to life.

It doesn't even matter that they're getting their asses handed to them; the opposing team has quite a go, filling up the bases, scoring a couple of runs before they can even manage a single out. When a burly woman steps up to the plate, Nathaniel sees the hit before it happens with the same inexplicable clarity he had earlier when he'd heard Freya's song and known that it was, somehow, meant for him. So he knows the hit will be a fly, heading straight to right field, straight to Freya. Before the bat connects with the ball, he's already moving toward Freya, who, when she sees the ball sailing toward her, crouches a bit and tentatively reaches her left, ungloved, hand to catch it. Nathaniel knows it'll bruise the hell out of her if she catches it and smash her in the face if she doesn't. He comes up behind her. "I got it," he calls, and loops an arm around her shoulder, easily catching the ball and sending it to the third baseman in time to tag the runner.

"Nice one," Finny calls.

"Yeah, nice one," Freya says.

"Anytime," Nathaniel replies.

A blast. A total blast.

How long since he's swung a bat? Caught a pop fly? Had butterflies in his stomach because of a girl? When he came back to school with his eye patch, his teammates treated him politely but coolly. They didn't make jokes around him anymore, didn't invite him to hang out on Friday nights. He went to every practice, sat on the bench.

When he got fitted with his temporary prosthetic eye—which became permanent by default—his coach invited him to the field, just the two of them, for a game of catch. Nathaniel caught the first few tosses easily, but then the coach threw a few higher and to the left. Nathaniel reached up with his glove to where he thought the ball should be, but came back with an empty glove. This happened again, and again.

The doctors had warned that his depth perception would be off. That certain things, like descending stairs, would be difficult, and other things, like watching 3-D movies, would be impossible, but over time, his good eye would learn to compensate. He told the coach this. He promised to practice round the clock.

"I'm losing most of my strongest guys this year," the coach said. "This might be our last shot at the championship for a while." He looked at Nathaniel, not saying any more. He didn't have to. Nathaniel realized what he was expected to do.

"It's all good," Nathaniel told his coach. He said the same thing to his teammates when he announced he was quitting. He tried not to take it personally when they all believed him so eagerly.

Now he steals glances at Freya the way he once stole bases. He's skilled enough at this that she doesn't notice, but when Finny yells, "Look alive, outfield!" just as a ground ball streaks past the second baseman, he realizes he hasn't been paying attention to the game at all. The ball is skidding directly toward Freya, too late for Nathaniel to intercept.

But Freya scoops up the ball in her gloved hand this time. "I did it!" she cries, turning to Nathaniel. "Now what?"

"Throw it to me," he calls, jogging toward her.

She does an underhand toss, which he easily catches. Then he pivots, throwing the ball past Finny, all the way to Harun. Two runners have crossed home, and the third is making a start for it and Finny is expecting Nathaniel to throw the ball back to him, but Nathaniel knows that today they all have a sort of magic on their side, so he beams the ball toward Harun, certain that he'll make the catch, which, backlit by the setting sun, he does.

"Out!" yells the umpire.

"Did we do it?" Freya asks.

"We did it," Nathaniel says.

Freya whoops and does a little victory dance. "Go, Harun!" She high-fives Nathaniel, and now his right hand tingles just as much as his left.

"Ha!" Finny calls. "Suck it!"

"Suck what?" the other team captain says. "We're up by four."

"Suck it anyway!" Finny replies, and then, emboldened with some mojo, proceeds to strike out the next batter, and that's three outs.

Their team up to bat, Freya and Nathaniel take their seats on the benches. Harun stands next to the chain-link fence in conversation with Finny.

"I'm not going to have to bat, am I?" Freya asks.

"There's a bunch of batters ahead of you, so don't worry," Nathaniel says.

"Because I don't know how to bat."

"I can show you if you want."

"I might smash you in the head. Again. Give you a second concussion."

"I'll take the risk."

They walk over to the bat bag, and Nathaniel rifles through. "First off, you need the right bat."

"What's the right bat?"

"For you," he says, extracting a slim wooden number, "it has to be a Louisville Slugger."

He hands her the bat, and she grips it like she's trying to suffocate it.

"Relax," Nathaniel says, coming to stand behind her. "Hold your hands one on top of the other, lining up your knuckles." He reaches over to adjust her grip, wrapping his body around hers.

"Like this?" she asks in a voice that's pure breath.

Her grip is just fine, but he doesn't want to let go. He's so tired of letting go. "Yeah, like that. Now open your legs."

"Usually guys buy me dinner before they say that."

Nathaniel's boner is immediate, and as stiff as the Louisville Slugger. He adjusts his body away from Freya so she can't tell.

"This wide." Nathaniel nudges her feet apart, willing his boner to go down. He hasn't been like this since he was thirteen. "The trick is to relax. Don't anticipate the ball, receive the ball."

"*Receive the ball,*" Freya teases. "Are we playing softball or having—"

"Nathaniel," Finny interrupts. "You want to bat?"

No! Nathaniel does not want to bat. He wants to take Freya into that patch of bushes and rip off her clothes and press up so close against her warm skin that there's no space between them. Afterward, he'll buy her dinner.

"Here, take the Slugger," Freya says, handing Nathaniel the bat, and even though it's too light for him, he takes it because he doesn't want to refuse this girl anything.

He stands at home plate, desire thrumming through him. The pitcher throws wide. Nathaniel could move aside and it'd be a ball, but instead he swings hard. He needs to do something with all the longing and craving and desire that he thought was dead but turns out was just dormant and is now volcanically erupting. The ball connects with the most satisfying of thwacks and goes flying.

Home run. Of course.

The three missing players show up at the end of the third inning, and Freya, Nathaniel, and Harun are dispatched with a gush of thanks, two beers and a Coke, and an invitation to return next week.

"I'd come back if you guys did," Freya says. "That was fun." But she remembers that Nathaniel isn't from here. He's a tourist, meeting his dad. "Will you even be here next week?"

"Maybe," Nathaniel says, shrugging as he pops open a beer. The foam explodes all over his hands.

He licks his fingers, and Freya thinks ten thousand filthy thoughts about what she'd like to do to, and with, those fingers. But before she makes yet another stupid sex joke, she takes a long chug of the beer and lets loose an equally long belch.

Nathaniel and Harun stare at her, both of them clearly deeply impressed.

"Me and my sister used to have burping contests," she explains. "Though with Fanta, not beer. I always won."

"Obviously," Harun says.

"I used to be able to burp 'Jingle Bells,' 'ABC,' 'Happy Birthday.' Hmm. Maybe if I can't sing-sing, I can burp-sing." Freya takes another swig of beer. "Can one have a career as a professional burp-singer?"

"Probably," Harun replies. "There are those guys who make a living as professional hot dog eaters, so why not?"

"Professional hot dog eaters?" Nathaniel asks.

"They compete. There's a big match every Fourth of July," Freya says. "That Japanese one always wins."

"Nope," Harun says. "He was disqualified."

"Really?" Freya asks.

"Yes."

"You're messing with me," Nathaniel says, laughing. "That can't really be a thing."

"It is," Freya says. "So maybe there's hope for me and my belching career after all." She drinks again and attempts to belch the ABCs, but all that comes out is a pathetically dainty *A*. "Nope. Can't even sing that way."

The guys look at her with a gentleness that's almost unbearable.

"I'm sure you'll sing again," Harun says.

"Are you?" Freya asks. "Because I'm not."

"Stealing the song didn't help?" Nathaniel asks.

Freya sighs. She knows that if life were a movie, she would've ridden down that elevator, holding hands with Harun and Nathaniel, and as soon as she'd spun out of the doors, out of Hayden's grip, she'd have burst into song. And they all would've danced. With jazz hands.

But she knows that's not how life actually works. Whatever boot has been stepping on her windpipe these past weeks is still there.

"It helped," Freya says. "But not like that."

"What will you do?" Nathaniel asks. Freya starts to give the spiel about fans and livelihoods and all she's worked for when Nathaniel interrupts. "Not if Hayden fires you. What will you do if you can't sing?"

Your numbers will drop. Your fans will forget you.

But that's not the worst of it. That's not what terrifies her or drives her. It never was. For all his expertise on fame, Hayden never really did understand this.

Maybe it's the beer or the adrenaline or the way Harun and Nathaniel reacted when she lost her shit in the diner or the way they're looking at her now. Or maybe it's the feeling, which has been growing stronger throughout the day, that she has always known these two, even though they only met today. But something gives her courage. Or maybe hope. Or maybe hope gives her courage.

In any case, she takes a deep breath and lets the monster out of the closet: "If I can't sing, if I can't do this one thing I love doing, this one thing I'm loved for, I'll be alone."

And there. It's finally out. The thing she fears.

— — —

The thing they all fear.

— — —

"You won't be alone," Harun says. "You have so many fans."

"That's not love," Freya says. "That's not lasting. I guarantee you that in time—months, maybe years—if I stop singing, even my most ardent fans will lose interest." Harun starts to object, but Freya waves away his protest. "Answer me honestly. Your boyfriend, as big a fan as he is, do you think he'd still love me if I couldn't sing? Do you think anyone would?"

— — —

Harun would like to tell Freya that James would never stop loving her. But if James can stop loving him, who is he to say? People stop loving people all the time.

— — —

"I would love you even if you couldn't sing," Nathaniel says.

— — —

Freya's heart stops.
　Or maybe it starts.
　"You would?"

— — —

I already do, Nathaniel thinks. But that's madness. That's his father talking, or the feral starving man inside of him, so once again, he remains silent.

— — —

Harun thinks he would love her too. Not because she is famous or because she can help him get James back but because she is her. He should tell her something—something reassuring—but he's too distracted by his phone. It is buzzing, the texts nearly constant, Ammi's urgency so profound, he can see her shoulders hunched as she squints at the screen, pecking away at the letters with her ink-stained fingers. R U OK? Where R U?

If Harun and Nathaniel can love Freya even if she can't sing, might his family be able to love him even if he can't be the person they want him to be? And even if they can't, can he let them continue to love a lie?

He pictures his whole family gathered around the table to honor a person he's never been. His words to Freya earlier come ricocheting back:

You must do things the proper way.

The proper way is not to trade one betrayal for another. The proper way is not to let the food on Ammi's table grow cold, to let her worry congeal into fear and then heartbreak. The proper way is to stop lying.

He understands why Freya is scared of being alone. It might sound crazy to some people that Harun, living among such a large family, feels that way too. But he's carried this secret since he was nine years old. And secrets carve fissures, until the fissures become trenches, and the trenches become channels, and the channels become crevasses, and suddenly you are alone, on a block of ice, separated from everyone you care about.

He has felt alone for a long time.

The odd thing is, today of all days, he has not.

THE ORDER OF LOSS
PART VIII

HARUN

I have never told anyone the whole truth. The closest I got was telling Amir not that I was in love with James but that I carried a flaw and I feared this flaw would bring shame upon my family.

"But why?" he asked me when I confided this over the phone the day after I'd sent him that Facebook message.

The phone line crackled between us, ten thousand miles the least of it. "I love the wrong person," I said.

He sucked in his breath. *"A gori."*

If only it were so simple as a white girl. Saif had already cleared that trail for me. "No," I told him. "Worse than a *gori*."

In the ensuing silence, I knew he was trying to figure out what would be worse than a white, non-Muslim girl. He could not imagine.

"Not a girl," I said at last.

The line stayed silent, but I could hear the change in his breathing and knew that he understood. In that moment, before he spoke, I did not care if he was horrified. I felt only relief. Someone in my family knew.

In a calm voice, he replied, "'Do not lose heart nor fall into despair! You shall triumph if you are Believers.'" It had been a long time since I went to mosque or read the Qur'aan, but I recognized the quotation. What I didn't know was if I could be counted as a believer anymore, having strayed so far.

Amir continued, "Do not worry, cousin. With Allah's guidance, I can help you."

"You can?"

"I believe I can. Do you want to recite the *Salat Ul-Istikharah* together?"

I had not recited the *Salat Ul-Istikharah*, the prayer we use to ask for guidance—or any prayer—in such a long time.

"Okay," I said.

We said the prayer together, and I immediately felt lighter, better. But that night I began to panic. What if Amir told my parents? What would they do?

I didn't hear from him the following day, and I texted, begging him not to tell anyone. He texted me back. And whoever fears Allah, He will make for him a way out and will provide for him from where he does not expect. And whoever relies upon Allah, then He is sufficient for him. Indeed, Allah will accomplish His purpose.

He will make for him a way out. I repeated that in my head. A way out. Amir would help me find the way out.

By the time Amir called again two days later, my calm had frayed as I imagined Amir telling Khalu, who would tell Khala, who would tell Ammi.

"Did you tell your parents?" I asked him.

"Not yet. Just my imam. He helped me come up with a plan."

"What is it?"

"Will you trust me?"

"I told you my secret."

"Will you trust me?" he repeated.

It didn't matter if I would trust him. I'd told him. I had no choice. "Yes."

"Be patient," he advised. "I will help you, but you must trust me."

"Okay," I said.

Two days later when I came home from class, both my parents were waiting for me in the living room, along with Abdullah and Halima. And in that moment, I saw my way out.

Ammi was crying, which was to be expected.

I took a breath, prepared to face whatever it was.

Abu embraced me. And for that second I truly believed they would love me no matter what. I thought that James was right: love could conquer all. And that Amir was also right: Allah would provide me a way out.

"We spoke on the phone with Khalu," Abu said, releasing me.

I stood back. *Be brave*, I told myself. *Be brave*.

"We are so happy!" Ammi said, dabbing her tears with the edge of her *dupatta*.

Happy? Ammi had cried for six months after Saif married Leesa. That she was speaking to me was a miracle. But happy? Something was wrong.

"Khalu told us what you want," Ammi said. "I don't know why you kept it a secret."

"Maybe because he's . . ." Halima began. She shook her head and looked at me with a hard stare. "Nineteen," she finished.

"Nineteen, peh," Ammi said, waving her hands. "I was that young when I married your father."

And she'll sing at our wedding, I heard James promise.

A feeling came over me, heavy and cold, like I was being covered in wet cement.

"I've spoken to your uncle, and yes, Harun is young, but it doesn't have to happen right away. And if it does happen quickly, he can live here until he finishes college," Abu said.

"And your father already looked at flights. You can go as soon as the semester is over," Ammi said. "But you will need to go straightaway to get your visa."

"I still don't understand why he can't find a girl here like a normal person," Abdullah said.

"Or why he's in such a rush," Halima added, staring at me.

"He wants to do it the old way," Ammi said. She looked at me with so much pride in her eyes. "He wants to find a bride back home and bring her here like your father did me. He's a good boy."

Halima snorted and gave me the dirtiest of looks. "Yeah, a good boy," she said.

"Oh, don't listen to her," Ammi said to me. And then she and Abu started talking about plans. It was like when they spoke Urdu. I could catch pieces of it, but not the entire gist. Dates. Brides. Visas.

My head began to understand what was happening, but not my heart. My heart had always had a hard time accepting reality.

"I know you told your cousin you wanted to do this as soon as possible," Ammi said. "But we have to wait to decide when. Or if the wedding is to be here or there. This depends on the family and the timing." Ammi paused to think. "And the girl."

"How will he know which girl is right?" Abdullah asked.

"He will know," Ammi said, smiling at Abu. "Your father met three potential brides, and I was neither the prettiest nor the richest, but he chose me. He said he knew."

"How?" asked Abdullah.

Abu paused to scratch his beard. "It just felt right." He looked at Ammi. "And I was right."

I remembered the first day I met James, when I'd been lost on campus and he'd asked me where I needed to be and I'd thought: *Right here is where I need to be.*

I'd known. Or I'd thought I had.

Abu clasped a hand on my shoulder. "I am glad you went to your cousin," he said. "But you could have spoken to me. You could have told me."

It was a small window cracked open, my last chance to tell Abu the truth about me.

I knew I would not take it. I was, after all, a coward. "I wanted to surprise Ammi," I said.

"And you did! Oh, you have no idea how happy this makes me and your father," she said.

Right here is where I need to be.

Not anymore.

The window closed. There would be no way out for me.

6

PLAN Cs

"*Beta*, is that you?" Abu calls as soon as Harun unlocks the door.

Harun gestures for Freya and Nathaniel to wait in the hall and goes to the kitchen, where Ammi can most often be found, but she's not there. He walks through the kitchen into the formal living room. Abdullah and Halima are sitting at the edge of the brocade sofa while Saif and his wife share a love seat. Abu sits in his high-backed chair. Ammi is, as expected, pacing.

"You're late" is Ammi's greeting. "What happened? Why didn't you call? Or answer your phone?"

Harun has prepared no lie, no excuse. Let the chips fall where they may. He braces himself. And then Freya and Nathaniel step into the living room. "Sorry we made him late," Freya says.

The arrival of Freya and Nathaniel, two total strangers, is so unexpected, it rearranges the atoms in the room. Ammi's worry turns to confusion. Abu's hospitality takes over. "You brought friends," he says, rising from his seat, hands outstretched.

"Yes, I brought friends," Harun says.

"*Friends?*" Halima says, eyes widening.

"Friends," Abu says, acting as if it's perfectly normal for Harun to bring people—one of them a girl—home without warning. "We will add two more chairs to the table. Come, Rabia, I will help you," he tells Ammi.

From the dining room, Harun hears the scraping of chairs, the clattering of additional plates and silverware, Ammi and Abu's hushed conversation, which he does not need to hear to know the content of. *Who are these strangers Harun has brought?* Suspicious. That's fine. That's why he brought them here. To subject himself to one of Ammi's scrupulous audits.

As the seats are rearranged in the dining room, questioning glances are bandied about the living room. None of his siblings say anything. They are too polite. It's Saif's wife, Leesa, who finally asks, "Are these your friends from school?"

And though he has not told Freya or Nathaniel a thing about this meal, or about his family, or his predicament, or himself, really, without missing a beat, Freya smiles and says, "Yes."

By the way Halima's eyes widen, Harun understands that he's not the only Freya fan in the family. He feels a twinge of regret that they never discussed this. It would have been nice to share *something* with someone in this family.

"What is it you study?" Abdullah asks.

"Music," Freya replies.

"Nursing," Nathaniel says.

"I didn't realize the school offered such a diverse curriculum," says Halima.

"Or that men could be nurses," Saif says.

"Don't be such a sexist jerk," Halima says. "Of course they can. People can be lots of things." Though she's speaking to Nathaniel, she's looking at Harun.

"Please," Ammi says, returning to the living room, "come to the table."

The table is set with the linens Ammi carried with her when she came here, nearly thirty years ago, and is laden with crispy samosas gleaming with oil, *pakoras*, jewel-colored sauces, *dahi bharas*.

They all sit. Ammi begins passing around the platters of appetizers. Remembering how hungry Nathaniel was before, Harun instructs Ammi to give him two of each, explaining what each one is.

When the platter comes to Leesa, she demurs and turns her attention to Freya. "Not to be rude, but how do music majors expect to make any money?"

Ammi coughs.

"I'm sure she'll find a way," Halima says, giving Harun a look.

"It's not so easy to make it as an artist," Leesa says. "When I was younger I wanted to be a figure skater, but there's no money in that either, and you have to travel constantly." She shakes her head. "I'm a homebody, so no thanks. Luckily, I had a plan B: real estate. You have to have a plan B. Do you?"

"No," Freya admits in a small voice.

"You should," Leesa says. "I mean, there's probably more money in nursing. And definitely in real estate. Steve and I do quite well for ourselves, don't we, babe?"

"There's more to life than money," Ammi says. "And many paths to take."

"So long as the paths lead to medicine, business, or law," Halima says.

"Don't forget," Abdullah adds. "Engineering is also okay."

"That's not fair," Ammi says to Halima. "You want to be a . . ." She waggles her fingers. "Cartoon maker."

"An animator, Ammi. Like for Pixar."

Harun watches this all in disbelief. Why are they talking about career choices?

Ammi turns to Nathaniel. "What kind of nursing will you do?"

"Stop questioning my friends," Harun says. He knows he's behaving rudely, but he wants the interrogation to turn from Nathaniel to himself, where it belongs.

"Hospice care," Nathaniel replies.

"With dying people?" Leesa says. "How depressing."

"I think it's an honor to accompany people as they pass." Nathaniel pauses to lick a bit of tamarind sauce off his finger. "We all die. It's the only sure thing in life and the one thing we all have in common with everything else on the planet."

"Indeed, but for us, may it not be for a long time, *Inshallah*," Abu says. "Shall we move on to the main course?"

Ammi stands. "*Beti*, help me carry in the food."

Halima stands. Freya does too. The three of them disappear into the kitchen, reappearing with enough food for ten extra guests. Freya sets down chicken *karhai* in front of Harun. "Your mom says this is your favorite."

Chicken *karhai* and lamb biryani and beef *keema*. All of the dishes are his favorite. But he did not come here for a nice dinner with his favorite foods. He came here to force the issue. Why is no one forcing anything?

"Is everything spicy?" Leesa asks, looking at the food. She turns to Nathaniel. "I always get the worst indigestion when I leave here."

"I made you something special, not spicy," Ammi says. She points to a bowl of plain spaghetti noodles.

Leesa grimaces. "I can't eat pasta. I have a gluten allergy."

"A gluten allergy?" Ammi asks.

"Yeah, no bread, no pasta, no cakes. That kind of thing."

"Saif didn't mention any allergy."

"It's okay. I'll just have rice."

"Try the lentils, babe," Saif says.

"Are the lentils spicy?" Leesa asks.

"To me they're not," Ammi says.

"What's *that* supposed to mean?"

"It means that she doesn't think the lentils are spicy," Halima huffs.

Leesa sighs. "How about we open that wine?" She gestures to a bottle, still in shiny Mylar wrapping, on the sideboard. "It's a twist-off." She turns to Freya. "I've learned from experience that this family doesn't own a corkscrew."

"We don't drink wine," Halima says. "Why would we have a corkscrew?"

"For guests?" Leesa says.

Ammi takes the bottle from the sideboard, holding it gingerly, as if it contains strychnine. "Do you want wine?" she asks Freya and Nathaniel.

"I'm fine with water," Freya says.

"Me too," Nathaniel says.

Harun looks at his friends, surprised at how at ease they seem. When he asked them if they wanted to join him for a family dinner, he didn't explain who would be there, or what dynamics to expect, or what the dinner was for. He didn't have to. They said yes as soon as he mentioned the meal, and once they were on the train, he couldn't figure out the right way to interject: *Oh, by the way, the dinner is a farewell for me because tomorrow I'm leaving for Pakistan to find a wife, even though I still love James and don't want a wife, and by the way, James told me to get the fuck out of his life.* That's not the sort of thing you just bring up out of the blue. Particularly if you are a coward.

Leesa stands up and takes the bottle from Ammi. "I'll just help myself," she says, and marches toward the kitchen. "You want any, Steve?"

"No thanks, babe."

After she leaves, there's another awkward silence. The Leesa fireworks dispensed with, Harun holds his breath, waiting for the main event to begin. For Ammi to take a close look at the ledger, to ask questions about Freya and Nathaniel and Harun's connection to them. Once that happens, everything will unravel, and Harun will have no choice but to come clean.

But Ammi just asks Nathaniel if he too is gluten free, like she thinks this is a white-person quirk.

"Definitely not," Nathaniel says, filling his plate. "What's this one?" He points to one of the platters.

"*Seekh* kebabs," Abdullah answers.

"And that one?"

"*Achar gosht*," Halima says. "Crazy spicy."

"Maybe start with the kebab," Ammi says.

Nathaniel takes three. Ammi smiles. "You have very nice friends," she declares. "You should've brought them home sooner."

Harun does not smile back. He did not bring his friends to impress Ammi. He brought them to activate her bloodhound nose. Surely his family would want to know what he was doing with these two people they've never met before. Surely Abu would be asking more questions than the perfunctory ones Leesa asked. Surely Ammi's curiosity about the uninvited guests would not be mollified by the sight of one of them hoovering his plate like there was no tomorrow.

— — —

About that.

Nathaniel can't stop eating. He's already full from the first round, but this is an epic feast. He's never had such an epic feast. Doesn't know if he ever will again.

And this food. He closes his eyes to process the flavors.

He has never tasted anything like them, but the flavors are still somehow familiar, even if he completely lacks the vocabulary to name them.

— — —

Freya can name them: garlic, cumin, ginger, cardamom, nutmeg, clove . . . spices her father used to cook with.

"Is there fenugreek in this?" Freya asks, pointing to the biryani.

Harun's mother lights up. "None of my children even know what fenugreek is, let alone how to discern it among the spices."

"It's used in Ethiopian food," Freya says.

"I've never had Ethiopian food," Harun's mother replies. "What's it like?"

"Lots of stews and sauces, similar spices. You eat it with fermented bread, using your hands."

"Back in Pakistan, we would eat this with our hands too," Abu tells her, before meticulously wiping his right hand and using it to expertly scoop up meat, rice, and sauce in a neat pocket of naan.

Freya watches him and does the same, only less expertly, and some of the sauce drips onto the tablecloth.

Harun's mother mops it up, waving away Freya's apologies. "I like to see people eat." She glances at the kitchen, where Leesa is still doing something with the wine.

"I'm out of practice," Freya says. "My dad's the Ethiopian, and he left years ago. My mom never liked Ethiopian food, so after he left, we stopped eating it." Freya wonders why that is. For the past few years, she has had plenty of money of her own, access to an entire city of tastes. She could've had Ethiopian food if she'd wanted to.

"But you remember the spices," Harun's mother says. "That part of you never goes away."

"I hope so," Freya says.

"You should cook your food from home."

"I don't really know how to cook."

"It's easy. I can teach you," Harun's mother offers. "I'm sure learning Punjabi food wouldn't be so different."

"I'd like that," Freya says.

"It's settled. You can come for a cooking lesson while Harun is away."

Away? Freya absorbs this news. Away where? She glances casually at Harun, but his face is frozen into a screen grab of horror. And Freya understands, suddenly, belatedly, that she and Nathaniel were not invited to this dinner just because.

"I have a favor to ask," Harun had said as they'd sat on the bleachers, watching Finny and his friends play the game. At that point, Freya would've done anything for either of these boys. And a family dinner didn't seem like a big ask.

"How long are you going away for again?" Freya asks Harun, her voice easy and light, not because she wants to know but because she wants Harun to know she'll play along, she'll keep him safe.

"Six weeks," Harun's mother answers. "I'll be so lonely. I'll need something to fill my time."

"Excuse me," Halima says. "Sitting right here."

"Yes," Harun's mother acknowledges. "But you don't want me to teach you to cook." She looks adoringly at Freya. "And Freya does."

"Freya does, does she?" Halima says in the universal needling tone of the younger sister.

"Maybe we can learn together," Freya tells Halima. For a second she forgets that she's just playing along for Harun's sake, and she imagines herself in Harun's mother's kitchen, the steam rising out of the pots simmering on the stove, a wooden spoon, dipped and blown on, for them to taste.

She glances at Harun, who looks utterly miserable. There's that yank on her cord, and Freya feels Harun's misery as keenly as if it were her own, even if she doesn't understand its source.

"If you learn Punjabi food, you can cook for your Nathaniel," Harun's mother says.

Your Nathaniel. Hearing Harun's mother say it, validate it, warms her. She cannot hide her smile. Doesn't even try. "Maybe I will," Freya says.

"He seems to like the food very much," Harun's mother says, watching Nathaniel wipe up any last smears of sauce with a piece of naan.

"No. I *love* this food," Nathaniel says.

"Not too spicy?" Harun's mother asks.

"I can take it," Nathaniel says.

"Not bad for a *gora*," Abdullah says.

"*Gora* is a white person," Leesa tells Nathaniel, emerging

from the kitchen holding a plastic tumbler full of ice cubes and, presumably, wine in one hand, the half-empty bottle in the other. "Isn't that nice?"

"It's not derogatory," Halima says, "just descriptive. Like calling someone a blonde."

"Complimentary in this case," Abdullah says. "Not everyone can handle Ammi's food."

"By 'not everyone,' you mean me?" Leesa says.

"I meant people who aren't used to spicy food," Abdullah says. "Like Nathaniel."

"Is that a challenge?" Nathaniel asks.

"Well, you haven't tried the *achar gosht* yet," Abdullah says. "If you can manage that, you will earn my undying respect."

Nathaniel helps himself to a ladle full of the mutton stew. Freya can see that the bite he takes has a small green chili in it.

"Wait," she calls out. But it's too late. Nathaniel's face is a three-alarm fire. He reaches for his water.

"No water," Halima says. "It only makes things worse."

Nathaniel ignores her, reaching for the water.

"You need yogurt," Harun's mother says, going to fetch some.

Freya glances at Harun, whose face is as ashen and pale as Nathaniel's is glowing, his plate as full as Nathaniel's is empty. If Nathaniel has noticed Harun's discomfort, he doesn't show it. She tries to catch Harun's eye, to send a silent message, but the shades are drawn.

When Nathaniel has cleared his plate a third time and everyone else has pushed their dishes away, Harun's mother rises to clear the table. "Please," Freya says, putting a hand on her wrist. "Let us do it."

"I couldn't," Harun's mother says.

Nathaniel stands and nods. "We insist."

"Harun? Help us?" Freya says. She wants him in the kitchen. She wants him back in the safe huddle of their trio. She wants him to tell them what's going on and how they can help.

But all he says is "I'll be just a minute."

Freya carries a stack of dishes into the kitchen. She means to share her concerns about Harun with Nathaniel, but when he comes to stand next to her at the sink, their hips touching, she's back in the park, behind the chain-link fence, holding the Louisville Slugger, Nathaniel so close to her she can feel every part of him, and her mind is a blank slate onto which she's writing loopy hearts.

"Hey" is all she can think to say, looking at his reflection in the window over the sink.

"Hey," Nathaniel says back to her reflection.

They rinse off the plates and stack them in the dishwasher. One of the bowls slips out of Freya's hand, and Nathaniel catches it.

"Saved me again," Freya says. "You've been doing that all day, it seems."

"And so have you."

"You seem to forget I fell on you."

"I didn't forget. I'm glad you fell on me."

"You said that before. Do you enjoy concussions?"

"No."

"So why would you be glad I fell on you?"

"Because it saved me."

"Saved you? From what?"

Nathaniel stops washing dishes, and even though he's staring at Freya's reflection, she can feel his gaze boring into her. The cord connecting them tugs tighter so there's no space left between them.

"From my plan B," Nathaniel says.

"What was your plan B?" Freya asks, her voice strangled in an entirely different way than it's been these past few weeks.

But Nathaniel doesn't answer. Halima appears with a new stack of plates. "You guys are making me look bad," she grumbles.

"What was your plan B?" Freya asks again after Halima leaves.

Nathaniel closes his eyes and shakes his head. "Doesn't matter. I'm on to my plan C."

"Being a hospice nurse?"

"Maybe," Nathaniel replies, looking at her dead-on. "Or maybe this."

And then he kisses her.

— — —

His mouth on her mouth. Her breath in his lungs. Nathaniel can breathe.

His fingers twining her hair. Her fingers clutching his hips. Nathaniel can feel.

His tongue against her neck. Her lips against his throat. Nathaniel can taste.

His groan in her ear. Her sigh in his ear. Nathaniel can hear.

His eyes open. Her eyes open. Nathaniel can see.

As Nathaniel kisses Freya and Freya kisses Nathaniel, every part of him that he thought was dead, that he thought no longer deserved to exist, comes roaring back.

One kiss. Nathaniel is alive.

— — —

"Are you guys almost done with the dishes?" Halima asks.

Nathaniel and Freya spring apart.

"Uhh," Halima says, coloring, stuttering. "My father wants to make a speech. So maybe . . ."

She looks back and forth between them, her gaze skittering here and there until it lands on Nathaniel, whose Louisville Slugger has returned with a vengeance.

Halima scurries out, looking at anything but them.

— — —

They start to laugh.

"I guess we should go back in there," Freya says, but she's

not sure she can. Her desire may not be as billboard-obvious as Nathaniel's, but it is literally making her weak in the knees. "I need a moment."

— — —

Nathaniel needs more than a moment. He needs all the moments. "Where's the bathroom?"

"Upstairs, I think."

He kisses her once more. More of a peck this time, hitting the side of her grinning mouth. As he retreats, his desire threatens to explode out of his skin.

"To be continued," Freya calls after him. "Later."

Climbing the stairs is painful, but it's the good kind of painful. The alive kind of painful. The plan C kind of painful.

Later. He hadn't considered the possibility.

— — —

Freya returns to the table, floating, melting, thinking the kinds of thoughts she ought not be thinking at Harun's family's dinner table.

"Where's Nathaniel?" someone asks her.

"He'll be right down," Freya replies, and the anticipation of his return makes her feel giddy.

"Dad, we gotta work in the morning," Saif says.

"Go on," Harun's mother urges. "We still have dessert."

"Fine, fine." His father looks at Harun, who is looking down at the table. "*Beta*, tomorrow you leave for the land of your family, to partake in a rite of heritage, and in doing so, you will enlarge our family yet again. *Inshallah*."

A chorus of *Inshallahs* echoes around the table. Harun's mother dabs at her eyes with a napkin.

"And maybe our family will expand again," Harun's mother says. "The table can always be set for more."

Upstairs, the floor creaks. Soon Nathaniel will come back down. He will smile at Freya. The dessert will be eaten, the dishes cleared. And then . . .

"So let us all raise a glass to wish Harun well," his father continues. "To hope he finds as good a partner as I did."

They all raise a glass, except for Leesa, who scoffs. "Partner? That's what you call it?" She turns to Freya. "Am I the only one having a hard time with this?"

Freya, still levitating five feet off the ground, doesn't quite get Leesa's question. Is she objecting to Harun being gay? "If it makes him happy, why should anyone else care?"

"See?" Harun's mother says. "They probably have this in Ethiopia too."

"They have it everywhere, as far as I know," Freya says.

"And I really don't see how it's your business," Halima tells Leesa. "It's his choice."

"And what about the girl? Is it *her* choice?" Leesa shakes her head.

Girl? What is going on? Freya tries to catch Harun's eye, to say: *Help me understand. I'm here to help. I can be your plan C too.* But he won't look at her.

"No disrespect, but between the burkas and the arranged marriages," Leesa continues, "the way you people treat women is barbaric."

"Babe," Saif begins.

"'You people'?" Halima fumes. "My parents had an arranged marriage, and they've been happily married more than twenty-five years." She narrows her eyes. "Let's see if you and *Steve* manage half as long. Because from what I've heard . . ."

"Okay," Saif says, standing. "Time to go."

"But we haven't had dessert," Harun's mother says.

"I don't want dessert," he says. "Leesa, meet me in the car."

"Gladly," she says. She stalks off without saying goodbye, taking the half-empty bottle of wine with her.

When the door clicks behind her, Saif turns to his family. "This is why we never come here. Because none of you accept her."

"Accept her?" Harun's mother says. "When she says such terrible things about us?" She shakes her head. "Why did you have to marry . . ."

"An American? Because I am an American."

"Someone who doesn't respect us," Harun's mother says.

"Oh, so we're all supposed to be like Harun? The good, dutiful son?"

"I'm not a good son," Harun mumbles.

"Please," Saif shoots back. "You're the same kiss-ass you've always been."

"Saif!" Harun's father says, an edge of warning in his voice.

Freya is paying half her attention to the squabble and half her attention to the sounds upstairs. A toilet flushing. A sink running. The sounds of footsteps on the stairs. Whistling. Nathaniel is whistling.

He's whistling and smiling as he enters the dining room. Freya tries to catch his eye to warn him that something is going down, but he doesn't see.

But she does. In sickening slow motion, she suddenly sees that everything's about to go sideways. She's felt this way before. And once again, she is helpless to do anything.

— — —

"I'm not a good son," Harun repeats.

"Of course you are," Ammi says. "And you're going to marry someone nice and bring joy to your whole family."

— — —

Nathaniel, who only catches the bit about Harun getting married, and who is drunk on that kiss, feels elation for his friend. And relief. All day long, a melancholy has radiated off of Harun, even when he spoke of his boyfriend, and Nathaniel wondered why he hasn't called this James, if something was amiss. He'd felt a kinship with Harun's sadness, with his secrets. But now it's different. Nathaniel has *laters*. And Harun does too. "So you're going to marry James?" he says.

— — —

Harun exhales.

There. There it is. At last.

"James?" Saif asks. "Who's that?"

— — —

The hospice nurse, Hector, once told Nathaniel that you could tell when someone passed because the air changed. "It's like the departing soul leaves a shadow behind."

No one has died, but Nathaniel feels the sudden change in the room. Where moments before there had been plan Cs and *later*s, now there is only emptiness. It's a feeling he knows all too well.

He snaps back to reality as he takes in the heaviness in the room. Harun's trembling hands. Freya's contorted face. Did he do this?

"Who's James?" Harun's brother asks again.

Nathaniel sees the despair on Harun's face. It's a look he knows all too well.

What the hell has he done?

— — —

"Is this James another friend from school, *beta*?" Abu asks.

When Harun turns to Ammi, her face is so hopeful, he almost wants to say yes.

School was where they met, after all. Harun was lost and James showed him the way. It wouldn't be a lie.

But he has just heard his father say James's name out loud. He won't deny him any longer.

"James is a boy," Harun explains. "A boy I'm in love with."

"But you're going to find a girl to marry," his mother says. "You're leaving tomorrow. Khala and Khalu have arranged it."

"I'm sorry, Ammi," Harun says. "I can't do that."

And in the hanging moment of silence that follows, as blanks are filled in, suspicions are confirmed, things unseen emerge from the corners, Harun believes that whatever happens next, it will be worth it.

He will make for him a way out.

"Why can't you do that?" Ammi asks.

The silence is awful. But Harun is powerless to speak. So it falls to Halima.

"Because he's gay," she says.

Saif guffaws. "Wait, Harun's a faggot?"

"Don't call him that!" Halima says.

"I don't understand," Ammi says.

"I know you don't," Halima says, patting her on the hand. "It means he loves boys, not girls. Like Assad Khan."

"The actor?" Ammi asks, more confused now.

"Yeah, and you know Auntie Zahra's daughter, Na'ila? She's gay too."

"All this time, you've been riding me because I married Leesa, but Harun's a *chaka*," Saif says, switching to Urdu. "I knew. I freaking knew it."

"If you knew it," Harun cries out, "why didn't you say something? Why did you make me bear it on my own?"

— — —

Harun's brother is shouting. And his mother is crying. And now formidable Freya is crying too.

Nathaniel watches in frozen horror. He did this. He doesn't know how, but he knows he did. Everything was fine and good and happy until he showed up, and now this family is splintering. In front of his very eyes. Like his own family splintered before his very eyes.

I did this, Nathaniel thinks. It's not the other people. It's him. He is the poison pill. He's the one who makes things fall apart, makes people disappear, one after the other. Turns it all to ash. No wonder everyone runs away.

Just us, buddy. Fellowship of two.

His father is the only person he understands, who understands him. The person who protects him. He's the only person he's ever belonged with. What was Nathaniel thinking? Weekly pickup games? Family dinners? Kissing girls like Freya? Plan Cs? *Laters?*

There is no later. That was the point in coming here. To do away with the possibility, decapitate the hope of a later.

His heart pounds, the earth opens. It's already swallowed up everything he knows, everything he touches. It's coming for him too.

He's so tired.

You're almost there, buddy.

— — —

Ammi is crying, repeating, "I don't understand," which is bad enough. But when Abu says, "You deceived us?" with an upward tilt, like a question, like he does not believe Harun is capable of such a thing, his defective heart breaks once and for all.

"I didn't mean to," Harun says. "I never meant for all this . . ." He gestures to the table. "I was trying to spare you."

"Spare us what?" Abu asks. He collapses his body over Ammi's body, to protect her, Harun realizes, from him.

"This."

— — —

Nathaniel snatches his backpack. The contents spill out. He leaves them on the floor, except for one thick book, which he grabs before bolting toward the door.

"Nathaniel!" Freya calls out after him. "Wait!"

Nathaniel doesn't hear her. He tears past, both eyes wide open and unseeing.

"Nathaniel!" Freya shouts. "Look at me."

He does not look at her. He does not see her.

Freya reaches out to grab his hand. He yanks it back, violently, and Freya loses her balance for the second time that day. Only this time, there is no Nathaniel to break her fall.

— — —

Harun surveys the wreckage of his family. Ammi has run upstairs, Halima and Abu following her. Saif is gloating. Abdullah won't look at him. Yet it is the sight of Freya and Nathaniel that threatens to undo him. Before this moment, Harun thought nothing could be as soul-killing as the look James gave him when he'd called him a coward and told him to *Get the fuck out my life*. But the way Nathaniel looks as he runs out of the dining room, pushing Freya to the floor—that is worse.

Who but a coward would employ strangers to do such dirty, dirty work? Who but a coward would imagine this is the proper way to do things?

THE ORDER OF LOSS
PART IX

NATHANIEL

You know that saying about a frog in a pot? How you can put a frog in boiling water and it'll jump straight out, but if you put a frog in tepid water and slowly increase the heat, it'll adjust and adjust until it dies?

Dad decided to try an experiment once to see if it was true. He caught a frog from the crick, put it in a pot of water, turned the burner to low. He stood over the stove, talking to the frog. He was convinced it would jump out once the water got uncomfortably warm, but it just sat there docile, swimming around.

When it stopped swimming, Dad pulled it out of the water and put it back outside, but it was already dead. He seemed surprised that he'd killed it. The water hadn't been boiling, just very hot. He got very quiet and broody, locking himself in his room for several hours. When he came out, he was ashen. "I didn't mean to," he whispered.

— — —

I realized that I was the frog in the pot. I had a lifetime to figure this out, but it took those two weeks on my own to realize I was cooked.

Two weeks might not sound like much, but you try spending two weeks alone in a house. Totally alone. No TV. No phone calls. No visit from the mailman. Nothing.

I did.

I thought the world had ended.

It had.

I waited for someone to come, to call.

They didn't.

Outside, the rain was unrelenting. Biblical. If it kept up, I thought the whole house would be washed away, swallowed up into a gap in the earth, leaving no trace of its existence. Only forest. And frogs.

Maybe that was how it should be.

A few years earlier, my father had watched some doomsday documentary and had gone into full-on survivalist mode, readying the house for all manner of catastrophe. He ordered a bunch of dehydrated food, jugs of water, canned juices and fruits, granola bars, industrial-sized vats of peanut butter. "Enough for us to survive for a month," he said.

I'd thought it was his usual impulsiveness. I thought it was Dad. I thought the food would collect dust in the basement for decades. I never thought I'd eat it.

But I did. I lived on that cache for two weeks. I'm not sure if I survived, though.

— — —

Two weeks alone in a house. It did something to a person.

All those years alone in a house with my father. It also did something to a person.

I could see that as I roamed the empty house, waiting for someone to call, to show up, to say my name.

No one did. Why would they? I was already dead.

— — —

As the rain continued to fall and the phone continued to not ring and the doorbell continued to stay silent, I went through my father's things. Without him there to put it all in context, to make it seem if not normal then typical, or at least *Dad*, I understood the water had been boiling for some time.

Under his bed I found the stash of mood stabilizers, the drugs Mom had insisted he take if he wanted to retain full custody after Mary died, the drugs I dutifully picked up at the pharmacy in town every month, the drugs I poured him a glass of water before bed each night to swallow down. He'd been hoarding them. For years, it looked like.

Next to that box was Mary's old suitcase. Inside were the notebooks where he'd written his theories, gleaned from the documentaries he'd watched over the years: The healing tree frogs and his absolute certainty that the cure to Mary's cancer was in our forest. The man who wrote the longest novel in history, discovered only years after his death, setting off a search for the thing he would create to leave behind after his death. The one about empaths, the one about suicide tourism, the one about the seeing blind man. There were pages and pages of notes, drawings, quotations. It seemed normal enough. Dad enough. Until I got to the entry about people who had learned to harness all 100 percent of their brains.

Dad had written pages and pages on this particular documentary. According to his notes, most humans utilized only 10 percent of their brains, but the people in this film had found the ability to access close to 100 percent and had accomplished superhuman feats like flying and learning dozens of languages. *If the doors of perception were cleansed, everything would appear as it is, infinite*, Dad had scrawled.

I remembered when Dad first told me that; it was the day we'd gone out into the forest blindfolded, in search of limitless sight. I knew my life had changed that day, but I belatedly understood that his had too.

A lot of the films Dad watched were rife with conspiracy theories, which was why I'd stopped watching with him. This one had sounded particularly outlandish—but also familiar. I tried to recall it, and when I did, I realized it wasn't a documentary at all. It was a science-fiction movie.

Not long after that, I discovered my father's copy of *The Lord of the Rings*. The pages were darkened with underlined passages, full of doodles and quote callouts, theories scrawled into the margins, epic ideas about the location of Middle-earth. Had my father lost the ability to distinguish between science fiction and documentary, between real and imaginary, between Middle-earth and Earth? Had he ever had it in the first place?

Fellowship of two.

Had I?

Just us, buddy.

It was hard to read the book with all his scribbles, but as the rain continued, I forced myself. I read it cover to cover, out loud, as my father had read it to me all those years ago.

It had taken him six months to read it to me. It took me five days to read it to him.

The rain continued to fall. The water continued to boil.

— — —

It rained the entire time I was reading. It was only when I got to the very end, when Sauron has been vanquished and Frodo and Bilbo leave the Shire, that the rain began to slow to a drizzle.

I paused for a moment at the last page. My voice was hoarse. My nerves were shot. My heart was broken. And for a moment I was transported back to the day when we finished reading the book the first time, before my mother left, before Mary died.

"Why does Frodo have to leave?" I'd asked my father, distraught about the dissolution of the fellowship. "Why doesn't Sam go with him?"

"Because Frodo was damaged in a way Sam wasn't," my father said.

"Why?"

"Because of the beautiful, terrible burden of the ring."

"Where is Frodo going?"

"To the West. To the Undying Lands."

"Does he go there so he won't die?"

"I think so he can heal."

"Can we go there?"

"Someday. If we need to."

— — —

I put the book down. I walked to my father's closet, ran my fingers over the fading list. The places were all there. New York City. Rivendell. Mount Denali. The Shire. Angkor Wat. The Undying Lands. Dozens of places, some real, some make-believe. We hadn't gone to any of them.

Next to the list was a mirror, old and scratched. I caught a glimpse of myself in it. I hadn't showered or shaved or even changed my clothes in two weeks.

I looked feral. I looked like a madman. I looked like my father.

— — —

The rain stopped. I called the airline.

— — —

I gathered up all of Dad's notebooks and went to the forest, to the place where we'd spread Grandma Mary's ashes, where we'd buried the birds we couldn't save, the frog he hadn't meant to boil, to the place where Dad had tried to find limitless sight and I'd lost half of mine. I ripped out a single page from one of the notebooks and laid the rest in a pile. I lit them on fire. The flames danced and hissed, the sodden earth steaming under them, and soon the notebooks, like everything else, had turned to ash.

I showered. I shaved. I changed my clothes. I emptied out the refrigerator. I packed a small rucksack with a few changes of clothes I wouldn't need, with Dad's copy of *The Lord of the Rings*. I put the key under the mat. I walked down the driveway for the last time. I walked two miles to the bus stop. When I boarded the bus, there were people on it, but I no longer felt like one of them. My axis had shifted. I was invisible. I was already in the Undying Lands.

I went to the bank and withdrew the rest of the money that Grandma Mary had left me. I went to the library and checked out an outdated guidebook I knew I'd never return. I threw my library card in the trash. I rode another bus to the airport. As the plane climbed above the trees, the clouds, the mountains, I didn't look down.

7

THE SWALLOWING
OF SECRETS

Freya tears down unfamiliar streets, past the buttoned-up modest frame houses, past the cemetery, its flowering trees ghostly in the quiet moonlit night. She calls out: *Nathaniel. Nathaniel. Nathaniel.*

— — —

In the silence that has descended upon the dining room, Harun hears Freya calling to Nathaniel. It mingles with the muffled sound of Ammi's sobbing upstairs and Halima's inaudible comforting words.

There had been so many of them before—his parents, his siblings, his friends—and now there's no one left but him and Abdullah, who is staring hard at the table, as if straying his glance even an inch will cost him something dear.

"Abdullah," Harun asks. "What should I do?"

His brother won't help him. He won't even look at him.

It is the thing he knew would happen, the thing he feared

would happen, being cast out, being alone. But just because he anticipated it doesn't mean he's prepared for it. The wallop of anguish is so powerful, it separates Harun from his body, so he's floating outside himself, watching from above as he picks up Nathaniel's discarded backpack, opens the front door to the only home he's ever known. Before he closes the door behind him, he turns back to his brother. "I used to want to be a pilot," he tells Abdullah. "Did you know that?"

Abdullah doesn't answer. Because of course he didn't know that.

— — —

Freya stops in front of a closed auto-body shop, momentarily disoriented. *How did I get here?* she asks herself for the second time that day. But then she remembers how. Harun, Nathaniel. She regains her bearings. She continues looking.

— — —

Outside, Harun walks down his block, past all the other houses, warm lamplight and the blue splash of TV spilling out of drapes. Houses holding families still intact. He hears Freya's sad lament: *Nathaniel!*

All day long, he has witnessed them fall in love with each other as he fell in love with them too. People think love can't happen that fast, but he loved James the minute he saw him.

"Nathaniel!" Freya calls.

Harun holds his breath, waiting for Nathaniel to answer.

— — —

Nathaniel does not answer. How can he? He cannot hear. He cannot see or be seen. His world has collapsed once more, a black hole sucking up all the space where light, where love, where *laters* might live.

There's just emptiness.

Just us, buddy.

As it always was. As it always will be.

— — —

Freya returns to Harun's house. Halima is sitting on the cement stoop next to the driveway.

"Did you find Nathaniel?" Halima asks.

Freya shakes her head. She didn't find him. She didn't warn him. She didn't even give him back his fifty-dollar bill, and now he's out there, alone and broke.

"Is Harun okay?" she asks.

"I don't know." Halima hangs her head. "I came downstairs, and he was gone. He's not answering his phone."

"Maybe he went to James's?"

"I doubt it."

As soon as Halima says this, certain things become clear to Freya. Harun has not spoken to James all day, in spite of the fact that she's supposedly his favorite singer.

"I think they broke up," Halima says. "I mean, I don't know for sure. He never told me. But I suspected that he was gay, and I suspected he was with someone, and once, I followed him into the city and saw him meet up with a guy."

"James?" Freya asks.

"I think so. But I never told him. Even when this whole marriage thing happened and I knew something had gone wrong." She puts her face in her hands. "But I never told him I knew he was gay. I let him bear it alone." She looks up at Freya, eyes so very solemn, so very much like her big brother's. "I think I failed him."

"I think I did too," Freya says.

Halima wipes away a stray tear. "I'm not supposed to be driving at night, but I'm going to look for him. Maybe he went to the PATH station. It's not that far. Will you come?"

"Or course," Freya says.

They climb into the car and crawl down Sip Avenue. The stores are all shuttered. There's hardly anyone out. It's like the night has swallowed everyone, and all their secrets, up.

When they get to Journal Square, Halima sighs. "Maybe it's better if I go home, in case he comes back."

"Okay," Freya says, not knowing where to go. "I guess I'll get out here. Maybe I'll bump into him on the train." But she doubts it. Finding each other like they did was . . . she doesn't know the word for it. Luck? Fate? Miracle? But she's pretty certain whatever it's called you only get so much of it in a lifetime, let alone a day.

"If he gets in touch with you . . ." Halima begins.

"He can't," Freya says. "We only met today. He doesn't even have my phone number."

"So give it to me," Halima says. "I'll text you his number

and give him yours. And you call me if you hear from him, and I'll do the same."

"Okay." Freya tells Halima her number. She opens the door to the car.

"If you see him, tell him . . ." Halima trails off, gesturing behind them, toward the quiet streets, toward home. "My parents need time. They thought he was going to Pakistan to marry a girl. They're in shock. But they love him. They just need time."

"Do you think so?" Freya asks. Did time heal everything? Or were some things broken beyond repair?

"I don't know," Halima admits. "But if they can get used to Leesa, they can get used to anything."

Freya chuckles ruefully. "Fair point."

Halima leans in to hug Freya. "I was looking forward to learning to cook with you," she whispers into Freya's ear. "I always wanted a sister."

"Me too," Freya says.

THE ORDER OF LOSS
PART X

FREYA

The first thing Hayden did after he took over was to quietly rename the Sisters K channel the Freya K channel, and a few months after that, to quietly drop the K. That was how easy it was to disappear my sister.

I continued to record songs and make videos, though now his team produced them. At first, they didn't look or sound so different from the videos Sabrina and I had made. They dropped weekly, on Tuesdays, same as always.

But with every new addition, Hayden deleted a couple of the Sisters K videos. If it was gradual, Hayden said, the fans wouldn't even notice. "Turn up the heat slowly," he said, "and the frogs in the pot won't know they're boiling." He looked at me. "Soon, no one will remember the Sisters K ever existed."

By that point, I wondered if my sister remembered I existed. Sabrina had not said a word when Mom announced that I would work with Hayden alone. She hadn't even looked that surprised, probably because Mom had consulted with her ahead of time.

She didn't say a cross word to me. Didn't accuse me of betraying her or selling her out. Didn't yell at me or call me a bitch. If anything, she was more benignly pleasant to me than she'd ever been. But two months after we inked the deal with Hayden, she moved upstate to finish college and didn't come home or speak to me after that.

Bit by bit, Hayden began to change the sound and look of my videos, nudging them—me—grittier by degrees, transforming what he dismissively called the "suburban cover artist" into someone edgier, more glamorous, more raw. "I'm not changing you," he claimed. "I'm revealing you."

We had lived in White Plains, but after a year, we moved to Williamsburg, which was closer to his office and more in line with my brand. Hayden had a furnished sublet we could have for cheap. Mom gave up the apartment I'd grown up in, and the family we once were disappeared entirely.

— — —

Hayden stuck to his two-year plan with the precision of a German train. After a year had gone by, a year of building my brand, getting me out there and visible, turning me into a commodity, we dropped the first single and took down nearly all the previous work from SoundCloud. "Gotta get your fans used to paying for the milk," Hayden said.

There were some fans who objected, who accused me

of selling out. Some even asked what had happened to Sabrina. *Has your sister died?* they wrote. But these comments remained in the minority as I was discovered by more and more new fans who had never heard of Sabrina.

I was the talent, I was told, because I was the voice. But, really, Hayden was the voice. Hayden made the calls. My look, my hook, my sound. He dictated all of it. When it came time to record the album, he hired a team of songwriters to create what he said would be a moody, atmospheric, and—without a touch of irony—confessional album. He employed a director who would shoot several videos simultaneously, to solidify the brand. "People want to see inside the real you," he said. "And we'll show them that."

He presented me a list of songs he'd chosen to record. Twelve of them were written by his team. But number thirteen was my song. It was "Little White Dress."

"Sing me a song that proves it," Hayden had commanded as soon as I'd closed the door behind me that fateful day in his office. Sabrina had just sung "Tschay Hailu," and when she'd emerged from Hayden's office, she wouldn't look me in the eye, dispelling any doubts I'd had about what she'd done.

"Proves what?" I'd asked him.

"That *you* are the only one I want," he'd said.

That was the first, last, and only time I'd sung him "Little White Dress."

"'Little White Dress'?" I asked Hayden two years later, looking at his list of songs. "How can I record that?"

"How can you not record that?"

He stared at me for one silent, squirmy moment. He didn't know the history of the song, other than it was the one I'd sung for him, choking back tears, all the while thinking that if Sabrina was going to betray me, I was going to betray her back. Had Hayden seen the bloody dagger in my hand? Had he been the one who'd given it to me in the first place?

"It'll need to be rewritten, of course," Hayden said, taking back the list. "But I do love that song."

— — —

By the time his team finished with it, the song was radically different. What had been just vocals and percussion was filled out with lush instrumentals. The lyrics had been rewritten so it sounded like an angry love song. The Amharic lyrics were gone. But the DNA of the song was still there. The melody was mine. And the story behind it—that was, for better or for worse, still mine.

We were three weeks into recording when it came up on the schedule. It started out as a normal enough day. I woke at eight, did some yoga, ate a light, nutritionist-approved breakfast, drank some herbal tea (no coffee on singing days because it was an irritant, though Hayden sometimes gave me a caffeine tablet to compensate). Did a baking-soda-and-water gargle. Self-consciously warmed up in the back of the car Hayden sent to bring us to the studio.

When we got to the studio that morning it was already

crowded—more so than usual. In addition to Hayden, his assistants, and the engineers, there were a handful of label execs and some other people I didn't know. Everyone was hunched around a monitor.

"Freya, look," Mom said. "They've mocked up a few prototypes for the art."

"Don't get too attached," Hayden warned. "They're just ideas."

I peered at the images. Body parts, black and white and sultry, the face half-showing. The name *Freya* in huge type. I didn't recognize myself. I'd been Freya Kebede. The Sisters K. And now I was just *Freya*, a menagerie of well-lit body parts.

"Let's get to work," Hayden said.

Usually we did a take or two to warm up. Then we began recording. Sometimes, Hayden would stop in between takes to give a note: *Go soft here, hit that note harder.* But this time, he kept shaking his head.

"Nope," he said over and over. "Not there yet. Not even close."

This kept up all morning. When it was time to break for lunch, Hayden waved everyone out of the booth and came into the studio to talk to just me. He didn't say anything for a while, just stared at me. I looked around for my mother, an assistant, anyone. But they'd left me alone with him.

"Freya," he said. "Look at me."

I made myself look at him.

"You're not giving me what I want."

"I'm doing what I've been doing," I replied. "So I don't know what you want."

"I want you," he said. "I want the real you."

But who was that? The girl who'd been born singing? The girl who'd betrayed her sister? The girl who could be the next Lulia? The girl in pieces on the computer screen?

"I don't know who that is."

Hayden tapped himself on the chest. "*I* know who that is," he said. "I've always known. It's why I chose you. So give me what I want."

"I just said I don't know what you want. More intensity? More growl? More volume? Tell me."

From inside the booth, I saw Nick, the engineer, return. He pressed the intercom. "We've got some pretty good takes, Hayden. She can maybe punch out a few lines and we'll get it in the mix."

"When I want your opinion I'll ask for it," Hayden told Nick. He turned back to me. "This song can't be done piece-meal, Freya. This song only works if we can hear your guts on a platter, hear your chest splayed open. So dig down deep and figure it out and sing me that fucking song the way you sang it in my office."

Hayden went back to the board, sitting beside a now-frowning Nick. I put my headphones back on and I sang. I sang that song to the bone. I sandpapered my voice, going back in time, year by year, through all the layers of varnish, through all the broken promises, trying to dig back to the girl who was born singing. I sang my voice raw, sang my heart to shreds looking for that girl. Did I find her? Had she ever even existed?

It was dark out when I finished the final, bloodiest take. Hayden came out of the booth, clapping his hands slowly. He was smiling proudly, almost, you might say, paternally.

"That," he said, "is the song that will make you famous."

8

THE SABRINA WAY

Freya has always known where to find Sabrina.

When her sister moved away to that college upstate, Freya looked up the school online. She spent hours on the school's website, picturing her sister living in one of the dorms, or taking notes in the lecture halls, or playing piano—if she still played—in the music studios.

When Sabrina graduated, Freya knew that she'd moved to the city, although the opposite side of it from her.

Freya has charted the route from her place in Williamsburg to Sabrina's Harlem apartment many times. L train to the A train to 145th Street. An hour, door to door, according to Google Maps. So even though she's never been there, she knows how to get there.

Outside the building, Freya's heart pounds in her head, a steady percussive beat. She looks for her sister's name on the buzzer, and there it is, *Kebede/Takashida*.

(She said yes!)

Someone is leaving the building, so Freya slips into the

vestibule without buzzing first. The apartment is on the sixth floor. The elevator clanks all the way up, *ba-boom, ba-boom,* echoing Freya's heaving heart. Her hand trembles as she knocks.

A man answers, tall, thin, delicate-featured, with a professorial air. Alex Takashida in the flesh.

"Can I help you?" he asks.

Freya is suddenly tongue-tied, unable not only to sing but to speak. Why is she here? Did she think stealing a song from Hayden, a song Sabrina always hated, would undo anything? Did she think a hug with Harun's sister would deliver back her own? "I'm looking for my mother," Freya finally manages to stutter.

Alex squints through his glasses at her. It occurs to Freya that he might not even know who she is. When Freya first met with a media trainer to practice how she'd talk about various parts of her life, she'd asked, "What do I say about my sister?" and the trainer had replied, "What sister?"

Does this man who is marrying her sister not even know Freya exists? Has Sabrina struck Freya from the record?

Has Freya not done the exact same thing?

"Of course," Alex says. "Come in."

Freya steps into an airy apartment, all hardwood floors, leaded-glass windows, views of treetops. A piano sits in the corner, sheet music and pencils on the desk. Unlike the apartment that she's been living in for the past year, which came furnished, towels already in the linen closet, plates already in the kitchen cabinets, a piano that has seen no fresh composition on it during Freya's tenure, this apartment looks like people actually live in it.

"Let me get Sabrina," Alex says.

In a different context, Freya might not recognize her sister. Her face has narrowed, her hair, always worn long, is cut into a pixie. It sharpens her angles. Shows off her eyes. She looks, Freya sees, more like their father.

"You're here for Mom?" Sabrina asks after only the slightest pause. She shakes her head. "How fitting. She's looking for you."

"Why?"

Alex and Sabrina exchange one of those looks, wordless but telling. Freya feels an ache, that age-old desire to have someone to understand her like that.

"She was worried," Alex says.

"But why?"

Sabrina frowns. "You didn't answer any calls or texts, and she tracked your phone and it showed you in Central Park, not moving, and then there was an Amex charge from an urgent care. So she thought maybe you'd been hurt. Or hurt yourself. She went to the police."

What? That doesn't make any sense. Freya's mother hasn't called all day. No one has.

Freya fishes out her phone for the first time, she now realizes, since she was back in the diner, several hours ago. Usually if she is away from her phone for more than a few minutes, her home screen has blown up with texts and alerts, but it's blank. She presses the home button and nothing happens.

She asks Sabrina to call her phone. Sabrina does, but the phone in Freya's hand remains dark. And suddenly it makes sense. "I, uh, dropped my phone in the park," she tells her sister. "That's why the GPS thinks it's there."

"You might've knocked your antenna loose," Alex says. "I can take a look."

"Oh, thanks."

Freya hands Alex the phone, and he hurries away with it, likely relieved to be away from the drama. Not that Freya can blame him.

"You should call Mom," Sabrina says, handing over her own phone. "She's frantic."

Freya shakes her head. If she calls her mother, she will wind up talking to her manager, and she's done being managed. "Can you just text her that I'm not dead?"

Sabrina taps at her phone. The response comes in almost immediately. "She wants you to call her," Sabrina says, reading along as the texts fire in. "Now. She says it's urgent. She says Hayden called and—"

"Stop!" Freya's voice is loud and firm, and for once Sabrina listens. "I'm not here to talk to Mom."

"I see." Sabrina puts down her phone and walks over to the dining table, upon which is an open bottle of wine. She pours herself a glass. "So why *are* you here?"

Freya doesn't have an answer. All she knows is that after all that's happened today, with the miracle doctor and with Hayden and with Harun and Nathaniel, she needs to be here.

"To congratulate you," Freya blurts. "On your engagement." To her surprise, the tidings are sincere. She is happy that Sabrina is happy.

Sabrina holds up her hand, the tiny engagement ring throwing prisms against the wall. She marvels—less at the ring, it seems, than at her own good fortune. "Thank you," she says quietly. She drops her hands in her lap. "Did Mom tell you?"

"Mom hasn't told me a thing about you in two years," Freya says. "I found out on Facebook."

"I didn't post anything."

"Alex did. *She said yes!*"

"Ahh." Sabrina smiles indulgently toward the room where Alex has gone to tinker with the phone. Then she looks at Freya. "Still stalking ghosts on Facebook?"

"Only yours."

Sabrina's eyebrow arcs in surprise. "Why?"

"Why? Are you serious? You're my sister. At least I think you're still my sister."

"I don't know. Am I?" Sabrina asks, her voice uncertain, as if she truly doesn't know.

This rattles Freya. She's used to the granite Sabrina. She came girded to confront that Sabrina. But she doesn't know what to do with this tender, unsure person.

"Do you ever hear from him?" Sabrina asks.

"Who?"

Her sister's eye roll is, at least, comfortingly familiar. "Dad."

Not Solomon, but Dad.

"Not for a while," Freya says. "What about you?"

"No. But I'm not you."

"What's that supposed to mean?"

"It means I'm not famous anymore. Or almost famous."

"Neither am I."

"But surely famous enough to get his attention."

There's pain in her sister's eyes, and Freya wonders just which one of them has been trying to get their father's attention all these years.

Freya shrugs. "I'm not famous, and if I'm almost famous, not for much longer."

"What do you mean? Isn't it all about to explode?" Sabrina blows out her hands, an identical gesture to the one Hayden made for them years ago.

"Mom didn't tell you?"

"Tell me what?"

"Never mind." She looks at Sabrina and takes a deep breath. It's now or never. "Why did you sing 'Tschay Hailu' in Hayden's office that day?"

The instant she sees the blood drain from her sister's face, Freya understands that she isn't the only one who's replayed that day over and over again. Sabrina stands up to refill her wine, filling a glass for Freya too.

"Do you know what Hayden told me in his office that day?" she asks, handing Freya the wine.

"How would I?"

"I thought maybe he told you." Sabrina shakes her head. "But then again, why would he?"

"What did he say?"

"He said I had a pretty voice, maybe even prettier than yours, and that I wrote a decent song, but that he wasn't interested in me, only you. I asked why. He'd just told me that I was a better singer than you, and we both know I wrote better songs. He was blunt. He said I wasn't interesting enough, wasn't special enough, and wasn't hungry enough."

There are tears in Sabrina's eyes as she continues. "And it wasn't like I didn't know. I'd seen how the fans reacted to you. Seen how much you needed that. But I was so pissed off. So I told Hayden he had it all wrong. You weren't hungry. You were desperate. That our father fed you a story about being born singing and then disappeared, leaving you nothing but that false legacy and a pathetic white dress. I told him that every song you sang, from that very first viral video to 'Little White Dress,' was really about you trying to get him back.

"He didn't know about the original video, so he asked what song it was. I sang it to him. When I finished, he looked at me and said: 'Where do you think hunger comes from? It comes from desperation.' And that was it. He thanked me. Told me I was very helpful. And I realized what I'd done. Hayden was a shark, circling you. And I poured blood in the water. But before I could fix it or warn you, he dismissed me and called you in."

"And I sang 'Little White Dress.'"

"And you sang 'Little White Dress.'"

"I betrayed you."

"Only because I betrayed you first."

"Have you ever heard that song, Sabrina?"

"Of course I have."

"I know you've listened to it, but I don't think you've heard it."

"What's the difference?" Sabrina rolls her eyes, skeptical.

The difference is everything. But Freya doesn't know how to explain it, so instead she sings what she can't say, sings what her sister can't hear.

> *You must confess*
> *I'm a white-hot mess*
> *And I need you here*
> *Need you near to quench my fear*

Freya's voice is strangled, as bad as it was that day in the studio, as bad as it's been every day since. She keeps going.

> *Did the thing I said I would*
> *Let music do what words never could*
> *You're a thorn in my side*
> *But loving you is how I survive*

> *All that I said I wanted*
> *Was a little white, little white dress*
> *All that I said I needed*
> *Was a little white, little white dress*

> *Do you remember? We used to sing:*
> *Eshururururu, Eshururururu*
> *Eshururururu, hushabye, hushabye, hushabye*

And though I obsess
'bout being a black-tar mess
I'd rather have you
Than a little white dress

The song sounds nothing like it did in the recording studio, nothing like it did on Freya's iPhone all those years ago. Nothing like it did when she first sang it to her sister, trying to sing what she could not say. *Don't leave me alone. I need you. I love you.*

But maybe this is how the song is meant to be sung. Because for the first time, Sabrina seems to hear it.

There's a tremble in her chin. Sabrina tries to tough it out, but the tremble becomes a wobble and then her stony expression cracks, revealing the human who's always lived underneath. "That song isn't for Dad," Sabrina says.

"No," Freya says. "It's not."

"You wrote that about me," Sabrina says.

"I wrote that about us."

Sabrina does something Freya has never once seen her sister do: she starts to cry. And Freya does something that, until today, she's never had the opportunity to do: she wraps her arms around her sister and comforts her.

It doesn't last long, because it's still Sabrina. She quickly wipes away her tears and disentangles herself from the embrace. "What the hell happened to your voice?" she asks, the question delivered in a typically direct and indelicate way. In the Sabrina way. And for this reason, it makes Freya laugh.

"I don't know," she says, cracking up. "I just lost it."

"You lost it?" The laughter is infectious, and soon Sabrina is convulsing with it too. "How'd you lose it? Did you leave it in a taxi?"

This makes Freya double over. "I don't know why I'm laughing," she says. "We had to stop recording. It's a total disaster."

"That's terrible," Sabrina says, wheezing for breath. "What are you going to do now?"

"I don't know," Freya admits, sobering up a little.

"Well, you'd better figure it out in two years," Sabrina says, wiping away an errant tear.

"What's in two years?"

"My wedding."

"Why would I have to . . ." Freya trails off as she understands what Sabrina is asking. Sabrina, who also never knew how to say things. "You want me to sing at your wedding?"

"Not if you sound like that . . ."

"And if I do . . . sound like that?"

The question hangs in the air, and Freya is terrified of what she just asked, what Sabrina might say.

And then her sister says this: "We'll come up with a plan B."

Something expands in Freya's chest. Acorns, after all, eventually bloom. They seed new oak trees, whole groves of them.

"Or even a plan C," Freya murmurs.

"Got it working," Alex says, emerging with Freya's phone. It's blowing up with the day's missed notifications. All her mentions, her views, her likes, her engagements, all her texts and emails and missed calls. There are several voicemails from Hayden she knows she will never listen to and dozens of texts from her mother that she will have to find a new language to respond to.

The phone continues to buzz with the things Freya mistook for love. Buried amid all the noise is Halima's text with Harun's number. Buried amid all the noise is actual love.

In the quiet of that moment, in the sanctuary of that love, something happens to Freya. She is lifted outside of herself, outside of this apartment, outside of her own loss and into Harun's. All of the stories he has yet to tell her—about airplanes, and Aladdin, and James—unspool inside her and become her own. Just as, she now understands, Nathaniel's loss has somehow merged with her own. It sounds like a burden, to take this on, but really, it's the opposite. To be the holder of other people's loss is to be the keeper of their love. To share your loss with people is another way of giving your love.

And suddenly, Freya *does* know what she's going to do. She's going to hug her sister and then walk out of here and track down Nathaniel and Harun, these two strangers who entered her life today and showed her what love really looks like. She has no idea where they are, but if Hayden Booth has taught her one lesson it's that if you want something bad enough, you find a fucking way to make it happen.

She's going to find them. The rest will sort itself out.

She clicks on Harun's number to open a text. Tell me where to find you.

THE ORDER OF LOSS
PART XI

HARUN

The last time I saw James was a beautiful spring day, as warm and soft as the day he found the fifty-dollar bill weeks earlier had been brittle and cold. The trees were in bloom. The women in the city had on dresses, and the boys wore tank tops that showed varying degrees of sculpted perfection.

We met that day in the park. James seemed happy. He was prattling on about getting his in-state residency after being in New York for a year and how he'd be able to start at LaGuardia Community College in the fall and how they had a food-service management program, which wasn't exactly what he wanted, but maybe he could transfer to the Institute of Culinary Education.

I only half listened to him. The day before, Ammi had assembled a list of gifts to buy. I had been fitted by a tailor for a formal *kurta*. My passport had returned from the consulate with a visa glued into its pages.

I emailed or texted with Amir every day. When I'd first realized what he'd done, I had been so angry at him: What had given him the right? Who had given him the right? But I realized that I had. By being a coward, by relinquishing control. And anyway, my cousin seemed so optimistic about the way things were going.

"Am I boring you?" James asked.

I startled back to reality. "What?"

"I been talking to you, and I bet you can't tell me one word I just said."

"Culinary Institute," I said. "Two words."

He shook his head. "You're distracted." He gestured toward the shirtless confections sunning themselves in the meadow. "If I didn't know any better, I'd say you were stepping out."

He was so completely off base—I'd never had any interest in the confections beyond the aesthetic—and yet completely on the nose. Because wasn't marrying someone else the definition of *stepping out*?

He'd been teasing, until he saw my expression. His face fell.

But he wasn't devastated. Not yet. He would not tell me that I'd devastated him—*ruined* him—for another few hours. At that moment, he thought I'd maybe hooked up with some other guy.

"Ja—" I began.

He held up his hand. "You still wanna be with me?"

There was nothing else in the world I wanted. I nodded.

"Then I don't wanna know. Do what you gotta do. I'm your first, and I plan to be your last, but if you need to figure out what it is you ain't missing, I'm not gonna stop you."

This was James. Giving me permission to be with someone else so I could be sure it was him I really loved. Because he was unselfish and brave and because he loved me.

"Just be safe, 'cause I don't want to catch any nasty-ass shit from some confection," he said.

"You won't," I said.

"And don't go falling in love, because that I can't take."

"I won't," I promised.

For the rest of the afternoon I let him think that I was having it off with some guy, and I let myself think that if he was okay with me hooking up with some guy, maybe he'd understand me being with some girl whom I wouldn't even hook up with—not that often, anyway—and whom I'd certainly never love.

After that we had an okay afternoon. We fell asleep in Sheep Meadow and got food from the halal cart James liked best and walked all the way to the top of the park, where hidden by foliage and ferns and caressed by the welcoming spring breeze, we loved each other in the ways we knew how.

James was normally chatty during sex, but that day, weighed down by what he thought was my infidelity, he was quiet. I, on the other hand, who was normally quiet, was so overcome with love and fear and anguish that I cried out.

"Just you try to find someone better than me," he said after. He smiled the saddest smile, and I knew that marrying a girl so I could keep hiding James from my family was not the same as hooking up with some confection.

"Next Thursday," he said as we exchanged one final kiss

under the cherry tree before he went uptown and I went home. "Park again, if the weather holds."

How easy it would have been to say yes. To milk one more day out of it. To come up with some excuse about why I'd be away for six weeks. To continue doing this with James for as long as I could. To continue deceiving him into thinking there was a future for us when I'd known, all along, there was not.

I put my hand atop James's chest. His heart beat strong and true under my fingertips—his open, loving heart, willing to shelter me and my secrets and my insecurities and even my infidelity. Willing to pay a price for things he cared about.

My heart was defective, not because it loved the wrong person but because it beat in the chest of a coward.

But even a coward has his limits. Even a defective heart knows right from wrong.

I moved my hands to the sides of his face, drawing him to me the way he had done that first time we'd kissed. "I have to tell you a secret," I whispered.

And for that one beautiful moment, before I spoke again, there was James's face, exquisite, expectant, all heat and warmth and optimism that the spring will return, that the sun will shine on all of us, waiting to receive my secret as he'd received me.

9

BROKEN HEARTS

Harun has always known where to find James. When he hopped from one couch to another, from cousin to aunt, Harun found out the location of the latest crash pad, committing it to memory. It made him feel better, knowing where to find him in case he lost him.

He could've gone to James's aunt's apartment anytime. He could've made some excuse for where he was going and taken the PATH to Manhattan, then transferred to the subway uptown all the way to the last stop, end of the line, James said, and walked the five blocks and knocked on the door and surprised James for no good reason except that he loved him.

But he didn't.

Until now.

His hand trembles as he rings the buzzer. There is so much he has to say to James.

That he has told his family, and it was every bit as bad as he thought it would be, but that he finally understands, maybe a little, what James meant when he said coming out to his father was worth the fallout. He'll never live down the terrible thing he made Nathaniel do for him. But the shame that has ridden atop his shoulders, an invisible and heavy stowaway since he was nine years old, has begun to, if not disembark entirely, at least pack its bags.

And that, as James might say, ain't nothing.

And he wants to tell him about Freya. About this astonishing day. Maybe he won't believe him, but Harun will play him the song that's tucked into his keychain, and when he hears that voice, he'll believe.

But mostly he wants to tell James that he's sorry. And he loves him.

He's buzzed through, and he climbs the stairs to apartment 3C. He knocks.

An older woman dressed in nurse's scrubs, wearing a lanyard from Presbyterian Hospital, answers the door. "Help you?" she says.

"Is James here?" he asks.

The woman, who must be James's aunt Colette, looks directly at Harun. Her eyes, Harun sees, are the same eyes as James's, brown and gold and warm—at least until she seems to understand who he is, and the suspicion rolls in like a cloud and removes all the warmth.

"You?" Colette says. "You him?"

Harun nods.

Colette walks over to the couch on which James is sleeping. "J," she calls. "Someone here to see you."

There's a split second when James wakes—pillow creases

on his beautiful face, puffy circles under his eyes—when he's still in that hazy limbo between sleep and wakefulness. Harun knows this place from the times they would fall asleep together in the park or in a quiet corner of a Starbucks or even on a subway when James would drift off. It would always take him a minute to emerge from sleep, to remember where he was. In that moment of in-between, Harun can see that James still loves him.

He blinks and it's gone, and James is awake and cold. "What you doing here?"

"I—I came to see you."

"I'll leave you to it," Colette says, touching James on the shoulder.

"I already told you, I don't wanna see you again."

"I'm not going to Pakistan. I'm not marrying some girl. I told my family tonight." The words tumble out in a breathless confession.

There's a flicker of interest on James's face, and his expression softens the tiniest bit. He nods. It's a start. "How'd that go?"

"As expected."

James nods again like he knows. Because he does.

"And I love you, and I'm sorry." Harun begins to cry. He takes a tentative step toward James and sinks to his knees. "I'm so, so sorry."

At first James stands stiff as a board, and Harun thinks it's over for him, but then he feels James's tentative touch on his head, hears James's soft voice say, "It's okay," and he thinks maybe it'll all work out.

James gently lifts Harun to his feet and says the words he needs to hear tonight. "I love you too." But it sounds different than it used to, mournful, and with a fist to the gut Harun knows there will be a *but*.

"But I can't be with you."

"Why not? I'm not marrying a girl. And I told my family. So I could be with you."

"Nah, boo. You told your family so you could be with your*self.* Live with your*self.*"

"I don't want to live with myself," Harun cries. "I want to live with you. To be with you. To fly you to Fiji and Brazil and all the places."

"You're gonna have to fly there without me."

"But you just said you loved me."

"I do. But you almost walked. No coming back from that."

"There is," Harun insists. "I'll earn your trust back."

James sighs. "You stepping out with some confection, I could handle. Some girl? Even that. But you were planning to *leave.* Without a word. I keep thinking, if I hadn't said something in the park, would Harun have even told me? Or would he have ghosted me, same as my mom?"

And it's at the mention of his mom that Harun understands that it's not the action, it's the deception. With James. With his family. James might love him and might even one day forgive him, but he isn't going to take him back.

"So all of this was for nothing?" Harun cries.

"Not for nothing," James says softly. "Just not for this."

James turns away from him. But no! Harun can't let him

go. Not just yet. "Wait!" he calls, yanking James back.

James's expression is so naked, his face so worn down by anguish, and it's seeing him like this that makes Harun surrender. To push James any further would inflict more pain, cause more damage. It would be the act of a coward.

And Harun wants, so very much, to be brave.

He unhooks the flash drive from his keychain and puts it in James's hands. *She'll sing at our wedding*, James once promised. "This is for you," Harun says.

James stares at the drive for a moment, but he doesn't ask what it is. He just closes his hand around it, nods once more, and retreats into the hallway. Harun hears a door close. The click is quiet and final.

Colette comes back into the room, looking at Harun with an almost painful compassion.

"You gonna be okay," she says.

"How can you know that?" Harun asks.

"When a broken bone heals, it's stronger than it was before the break," she replies. "Same holds true for broken hearts."

Harun nods. Prays this is true. Of his own heart. Of James's and Ammi's and Abu's.

Colette opens the door, gestures that it's time for Harun to leave. "Go be with your people," she tells him.

As he walks down the stairs, back into the moonlit night, he wonders: Who are his people? James? Not anymore. His family? Maybe one day again, but not yet.

Overhead, he hears the sound of a jet, and looks up to see a 737 circling toward LaGuardia Airport, and for a brief instant he's still the boy he once was, no secrets, only love. He blinks his eyes and then it's Nathaniel he sees, arriving, that very morning, on a jet like the one above, all secrets, so little love.

There's a yank on the cord around his heart, a reckoning in his bones.

He flips open Nathaniel's phone. He will call his father, speak to Nathaniel, reassure him he did nothing wrong. He will help him track down Freya, so they can continue to fall in love. It is the least he can do.

But it's peculiar. There are no contacts in the phone except for one. He checks the call log. There are dozens of outgoing calls, all to that one number. He dials and gets Nathaniel's father's *tell me something good* greeting. He hangs up and tries the incoming call log, but there's just one number. He dials it and is connected to an automatic greeting for the Skagit County Medical Examiner's Office.

He hangs up the phone and opens the guidebook. A slip of paper falls out. Harun picks it up and reads.

Mt. Fuji
Prince Edward Viaduct
Golden Gate Bridge
George Washington Bridge
80 MPH. Quickest way to die.

At first, he doesn't understand the meaning of Nathaniel's father's note, only that reading it rattles a knowledge that already resides in his bones, the same way his own secret has always lived in his heart. The flash of anguish that tears through him is different from the fear and uncertainty he's lived with for so long. It pushes him out of himself and when he returns, everything has gone quiet and still, and in that moment it all becomes clear. The vague destination near 175th Street, the father who never called back.

"As'alu Allah al 'azim rabbil 'arshil 'azim an yashifika."

The prayer comes to his lips automatically. He asks God to help Nathaniel. To help him find Nathaniel. To help him find Freya. To help all three of them heal one another. Because Nathaniel and Freya, *they* are his people. They are one another's people.

When his phone buzzes, he knows without looking who it's from, knows that this prayer God has answered.

He reads Freya's text. He tells her where Nathaniel is.

And then he starts to run.

THE ORDER OF LOSS
PART XII

NATHANIEL

The night I found my father on the kitchen floor, I had the most powerful déjà vu.

At first I thought that it was because Dad was lying not far from where Grandma Mary had been lying when she'd collapsed all those years before.

Later, after the paramedics came, not even trying to resuscitate Dad or pump his stomach because what was the point, after I found the hoard of pills in a shoebox under the bed, I understood that the reason seeing my father lying dead on the kitchen floor felt like it had happened before was because I'd been imagining it all my life.

I'd imagined it when Mom left and I was too young to know what I was imagining.

I'd imagined it when Grandma Mary died.

I'd imagined it when we buried the baby birds and the dead frog. I'd imagined it when I'd seen him weeping in the hospital after I came out of surgery. I'd imagined it every time I walked through the door after school, saw Dad on the couch, with the TV on, and exhaled a breath I'd been half holding since I'd left that morning.

I'd imagined it every time he told me, "It's just us, Nat. A fellowship of two." It was why I didn't leave. I thought if I left—for college, for Mom, for a life—I'd find my father, one day, on the kitchen floor.

So I stayed. And in the end, I found him on that kitchen floor anyway.

Déjà vu.

After the paramedics took Dad away, I waited for the calls to come. After Grandma Mary, that's what had happened. People came. Her church friends. My cousins. People.

But the only person who called in those two weeks was the coroner giving me the toxicology report, which she called "inconclusive." There were opioids and benzos in Dad's blood, not huge amounts, not drug-abuse amounts or amounts that suggested this was intentional, but sometimes, the coroner explained, even small doses interact in unexpected ways. "We're listing the cause of death as accidental overdose," she told me.

Inconclusive. Accidental. What did that mean?

"What do you want us to do with the body?" she asked.

I had no idea. When Grandma Mary died, Hector had facilitated everything. He'd called the coroner and looked up her life insurance policy and arranged it with the mortuary. I knew at the time that he was doing something my father should be doing, behaving the way a father should behave.

"Just part of my job," Hector had said, though I'd recognized this as the kindest sort of lie. He'd stayed until late that night, and he'd returned the next day, even though we weren't on his rotation anymore. "I'm moving back to New York City at the end of the year," he told me, pressing his business card into my hand. "But you can call me anytime. I put my personal cell number on the back of the card. You can always get me on that." I palmed the card, thinking he was being nice, and he was, but in retrospect I understood Hector realized I was a frog in a pot long before I did.

"I don't know what to do with the body," I told the coroner.

The coroner explained options, the cheapest of which was cremation. Did my father have life insurance? she wanted to know.

"Was it on purpose?" I asked.

Another pause. "We're listing the cause as accidental overdose," she replied. "You should still be able to collect his life insurance if he has it."

That wasn't what I was asking.

"Was it on purpose?" I repeated, my voice starting to break. "I need to know."

"We can't divine intention, but we are listing it as an accidental overdose."

"Did he do it on purpose?"

The silence on the phone was terrible because it was so familiar. It was that lag between people asking you if you were okay and waiting to hear that you were fine.

"Sometimes," she began falteringly, "it's better to just leave these things be."

"How do I do that?"

"Well," she said, "you just do."

She paused again. I could hear how itchy she was to get off the phone. This wasn't her job. She was not a grief counselor or a psychologist. She was a coroner calling with the good news that I could collect Dad's nonexistent life insurance. She wanted me to tell her it was all good. It's what everyone wanted me to tell them. Though they must've known it wasn't all good. How could it be *all* good?

"Do you have someone you might call?" she asked.

Who? My mother? The last time we'd spoken was four years ago when I'd told her that I no longer wanted to see her. The reason I gave was not that I'd lost an eye and was afraid she'd make me lose my father but that I didn't fit in her life and, more to the point, she didn't fit in mine. She'd cried bitterly, accusing me of always loving my father more. I didn't disagree. And I hadn't heard from her since. She didn't even know that the man with whom she had created me was gone.

Who else should I call? My coach, who'd kicked me off the team? My friends, who, having procured assurances of it being all good, had wasted little time in getting the hell away?

Hector, who had taken pity on me and had seen, in a way few others had, how it was with me and my father? But that was years ago, and anyway, he didn't live here anymore. And what if he did what the rest had done? Asked me, with impatience in his voice, if I was going to be okay. That I couldn't bear.

And anyhow, there was only one person I wanted to call.

Tell me something good, he said when I called over and over again.

But I had nothing good to tell.

Just us, buddy.

Not just us. Just me.

10

JUST US

Nathaniel has no idea where to find his father. He has no idea if Hector is right and he'll find him in that space between life and death, where the departed appear to escort the dying. Or if they'll meet in the afterlife. If there is an afterlife. Or maybe even in the Undying Lands, one of the many impossible places his father promised they would go together. Will he know the truth in the split second that separates life from death? Will it make a difference?

Will it hurt?

A body coming off this bridge hits the water at eighty miles per hour. *Quickest way to die,* his father had written in his notes.

God, he hopes so.

He prays it won't hurt.

He's hurt enough for one lifetime.

He stands at the edge of the bridge, crying. He's crying because it's cold and it's windy and his head hurts and because he's scared. He's crying because his father left him, maybe on

purpose, maybe not knowing any better, and now he's staring into the inky abyss, hoping to find him there, but he sees
nothing but more darkness.

But mostly he's crying because in the course of one day,
he's glimpsed the life he never had, the life he would've liked
to have, the life he can't have because of the life he did have.

He doesn't want to die. This was never about wanting to
die. But he can't be alone anymore.

He's been alone for too long.

Not just those unbearable two weeks, but the years before. He and his dad in the house in the woods. *Just us.* Their
fellowship of two has rendered him incapable of living amid
the rest of the world. Today proves that. Harun's face proves
that. Even Freya's kiss proves that.

It's not never having things that hurts. It's having them
and not having them at the same time. It's having a best
friend for a father. And having a lunatic for a father. It's having
a mother who loves you. And having a mother who deserts
you. It's having always known people like Freya and Harun
were out there but being unable to reach them.

"Dad, are you here?" he shouts into the empty night.
"Can you see me?"

There's no answer save for the rumble of traffic below
and, beyond that, the sound of a river, still wild, even here.

In his hand he holds all he has left, his father's copy of *The
Lord of the Rings.* When his father had declared them a fellowship of two, he'd felt anointed. A holy mission.

He was seven years old. Too young to know that there's

no such thing as a fellowship of two. A fellowship is a group. An army. A mass. Two people aren't enough. Two people can't save each other. How many times did he hear stories about one person drowning and the other person trying to help, but they drag each other down? It happens all the time.

Nathaniel screams to the void as he claws at the pages of the book. The binding's so old and creased and the glue is weak, but the book refuses to give. He manages to tear only a small handful of pages from the spine.

The pain feels like it is cleaving him in two. What is so wrong with him? What has rendered him so unlovable? So invisible?

"Dad, do you see me?" he screams. "Do you see what you did to me? Why?"

In the silence that follows, Nathaniel understands he's asking the wrong person the wrong question. It's not why his father did this to him. It's why everyone else stood by and let him. His father didn't know any better. But what about everyone else? Why didn't anyone turn off the stove? Gently lift him from the pot and lay him on the soft, leafy ground before it was too late?

Nathaniel grips the book, the seed of their sick fellowship, and with every ounce of will left in him, he hurls it. In the light of the moon, he watches the pages flutter as the book sails higher in the air than the physical laws of the universe dictate it should and descends not at a painful eighty miles per hour but gently, slowly, as if gravity has, for this one moment, reversed itself, allowing Nathaniel to back up and imagine his life with a different kind of fellowship.

In this version, Nathaniel plays softball once a week on a grubby patch of grass with people who already know his name. In this version, Nathaniel is seated at a large dining table, not eating buttered noodles with one other person but sitting with whole groups of people, eating foods whose names he does not yet know, but whose flavors he has always known. In this version, Nathaniel is not leaping to his own death but gently escorting others when it's their time, as Hector had done with Mary, helping them say the things they need to say while there's still breath, helping those left behind grapple with the questions he knows are sometimes unanswerable. In this version, he's kissing a girl whose voice he can hear even when she's not singing.

In this version, Nathaniel is not alone.

Because today, Nathaniel was not alone.

None of them were. Not after they found each other.

He's too far up to hear the book splash, but he knows the instant it makes contact with the water, because at that moment a sob escapes from the deepest part of him, and when it does a thousand pounds of sorrow—more than a lifetime of it—flow out of him. Was this how Frodo felt when Gollum finally fell into Mount Doom, destroying the ring, relieving him, once and for all, of the beautiful, terrible burden?

Nathaniel steps away from the railing. He won't see his father tonight. He might never see his father again. Might never know why he left their fellowship of two, or why he created it in the first place. Maybe his father didn't know that a fellowship of two is too small. You need more people. Mothers who you will forgive and who will forgive you back, wise hospice nurses who will teach you to escort people to the Undying Lands, teammates who won't care if you can only see with one eye because they'll know that the trick to a good catch is seeing the ball in your mind's eye. You need people who will give you the food from their plate because they feel your hunger, who will refuse to let you wander off alone no matter how many times you say it's all good, who will snap in your face and whisper so softly in your ear, *Nathaniel, come back, come back*, until you do.

Nathaniel, Nathaniel.

He hears her voice. Even with his eyes closed, he would know that voice. He's been hearing it since that day in the forest.

Nathaniel, Nathaniel.

He opens his eyes and sees Freya and Harun running toward him.

Nathaniel, Nathaniel.

If that's not singing, Nathaniel doesn't know what is.

Nathaniel, Nathaniel.

They see him.

He hears them.

They find each other.

ACKNOWLEDGMENTS

As with any book, many people pitched in to help with *I Have Lost My Way*, but I'm not sure it would even exist had Ken Wright, Anna Jarzab, and Michael Bourret not helped me find my way. Ken patiently and humanely held my hand through my crisis (crises) of confidence and several misfires, until I found my own voice again. Anna read an early train wreck of a draft and convinced me that these kids had already burrowed into her heart and that their stories were worth telling and then spent hours (literally) helping me figure out what those stories were. And Michael believed in me when I was unable to believe in myself. I would refer Freya to him if he represented musicians (and if she were, you know, real).

Thank you to everyone at Penguin Young Readers, with special shout-outs to Jen Loja for captaining the ship, to Leila Sales for fixing the words, to Elyse Marshall for spreading the word, to Kristin Gilson for making me sound like I play softball, and to Theresa Evangelista for the stunning jacket. Added hugs and thanks to Erin Berger, Rachel Cone-Gorham, Christina Colangelo, Aneeka Kalia, Emily Romero, Elora Sullivan, Felicity Vallence, Caitlin Whalen, and to all the sales reps who are on the front lines of getting books out there.

Thank you, thank you to my small army of readers who made me think harder, dig deeper, recognize my blind spots, and helped me get ever closer to something resembling truth: Imam Shair Abdul-Mani, Arvin Ahmadi, Libba Bray, Tamara Glenny, Marjorie Ingall, Farah Janjua, Justine Larbalestier, and Jacqueline Woodson.

Thank you to the members of LadySwim™ for support, sisterhood, and steam. Thank you to the Brooklyn Mama (and Papa) Brigade for being my hometown family. Thank you to my parents, siblings, and in-laws for being my family family. Special shout-out to my hospice-nurse sister Tamar Schamhart for inspiring the character of Hector. Thank you to Yosef Ayele for being part of my Ethiopian family. Thank you to Isabel Kyriacou for your ferocity. Thank you to Lauren Walters for All The Things. Thank you to Eric Gordon for ten years of this. Thank you to Lauren Abramo, Kieryn Ziegler, and everyone else at Dystel, Goderich & Bourret.

Thank you to all the booksellers, librarians, and teachers who put these little empathy-delivery devices we call books into readers' hands. We need you now, more than ever.

Thank you to all the readers, for being large-hearted and curious and willing to enter other people's experiences in fiction. We need that now, more than ever.

Thank you to Nick, Willa, and Denbele, for inspiring me, constantly, to do better and be better, and for being my fellowship, my family.